FUGITIVE LOVE

Julie wanted to be a good television journalist, so she was delighted when the chance came to go to Rumania with a fleet of aid lorries. She set off excitedly with Jan and Dieter, the two men who were to lead the expedition. But what started out as an adventure for Julie soon turned into a very dangerous journey when she became involved with arms-dealing and desperate rebels. And could she really trust the mysterious Jan Sometski?

Books by Dee Wyatt
in the Linford Romance Library:

THE GOLDEN WEB

DEE WYATT

FUGITIVE LOVE

Complete and Unabridged

LINFORD
Leicester

First published in Great Britain

First Linford Edition
published 1997

British Library CIP Data

Wyatt, Dee
Fugitive love.—Large print ed.—
Linford romance library
1. English fiction—20th century
2. Large type books
I. Title
823.9′14 [F]

ISBN 0–7089–5033–7

Published by
F. A. Thorpe (Publishing) Ltd.
Anstey, Leicestershire

Set by Words & Graphics Ltd.
Anstey, Leicestershire
Printed and bound in Great Britain by
T. J. Press (Padstow) Ltd., Padstow, Cornwall

1

"**W**HAT have you told him?" Colin Stiller's question was guarded. He sat with his feet resting on a low table and his eyes skimming over the copy for next week's documentary spread across his lap.

On the surface he seemed relaxed enough, but, deep down, he was living the kind of moment a father dreads. The moment when his only daughter receives her first marriage proposal. He felt uncomfortable. He had never stopped her doing anything before and he didn't want to start now, but he didn't want her to make a mistake either! Mark Brown would never be Stiller's choice!

The girl laughed, pushing a lock of blonde hair from her face, devilment in her blue eyes — as if this wasn't at all serious! "What a question, Dad," she

1

answered. "What do you think I told him?"

"How should I know? When do you confide in me these days?" He waited nervously. He felt she had no right to tease him like this.

Julie Stiller made a small tutting sound and glanced at her watch. She rose from her chair, her movement exposing a length of graceful leg and she grinned again at her father. "Don't worry, Dad. I told him no! I like Mark, but I'm not ready to settle down yet and I think he has the sense to know that." She laughed and patted the top of his head. "I've no intention of getting married to anyone yet! I've far too much to do before I settle down."

"I'm glad to hear it." Stiller pressed the top of a ballpoint and signed the copy. He slotted it into a folder and glanced narrowly at his daughter. "I have to admit that I'm glad," he said quietly. "I don't think he's right for you."

"Don't you?" She wasn't going to ask

why. Colin and she were close enough to share many of the same opinions. After all, the two of them had been alone together since her mother had died and Julie had never kept anything from him. She certainly wasn't going to start now.

Colin Stiller stood up, walked to the table and flicked through the morning's post. Relief washed over him. He hadn't wanted to pry and he was sorry he'd had to bring it up. The good relationship he shared with his daughter was something he prized and he didn't want to spoil it. Julie had always had a mind of her own but, if she had said yes to Mark Brown, he would have fought it tooth and nail. He wanted someone different for Julie. Someone who could love her as he did.

Julie smiled. "Let's forget it, shall we?"

"We'll do that," Stiller said. He grinned at Julie now, thinking again how like her mother she'd grown. And how the pretty kid with the long, fair pigtails and bright, blue eyes had grown into such a beauty!

Julie's next question came quietly. "Have you thought any more about my trip?"

Stiller picked up another sheet of copy and, inwardly, he grimaced. He knew what was coming and played for time. "What trip?"

"You know very well what I'm talking about."

He looked amused. "Do I?"

Julie's mouth tightened stubbornly. "Don't play games with me, Dad, it doesn't suit you. I've made up my mind. And if I'm ever going to be taken seriously as a TV journalist then I need something like this before I get too old."

"Too old at twenty-three? Rubbish! Besides, you are taken seriously. What would the company do without your research? Not to mention the way you look after your poor, old dad."

Julie laughed. "Poor, old dad? That's rich! You don't need anyone to look after you — especially me!" Then she threw a small, pleading glance at her father and became serious once more. "But you know what I mean, don't you? I promised Grandpa that if I ever got the chance, I would go to see Uj-Moldova for myself . . . perhaps put some flowers on great-grandmother's grave." She smiled up at her father. "And it would make marvellous copy, wouldn't it? I'm not just being selfish, you know."

Colin Stiller gave his daughter a fond look. "I know, I know," he conceded. "I remember your promise, too. Although, at the time you made it, I never dreamed that you would ever be able to keep it. Your grandpa has a lot to answer for."

"I have to see the place for myself, Dad — not only for Grandpa's sake. And now that the barriers are down, there's nothing to stop me, is there?"

Colin shook his greying, crew-cut head grimly. "It's still very dangerous out there, Julie!"

Julie Stiller raised sceptical eyebrows. "Now you're not playing fair! Moldova is no more dangerous than most places these days."

Stiller gave her a considering glance. "I'd still rather you'd leave it until all this border trouble settles down."

"If it ever does!" Then her expression changed to a bolder, more defiant one as she tried another tack. "At least it will get me away from Mark."

"Eastern Europe is more of a threat than any boyfriend of yours could be, dear."

Julie was silent for a moment, then she went on in a low, teasing voice, "You can't believe that, Dad. Moldova is infinitely more preferable than taking on a new son-in-law." She slipped her arm through his, cajoling him now just as successfully as she had done when she was his little girl. "Don't you agree?"

"Perhaps there's something in that!" he teased back. Then he squeezed her hand and added, "Why did your mother and I have to produce a daughter with such itchy feet?"

"Because, Dad," Julie said as she grinned back, "I take after you! And because," she went on, pressing her point home and sensing her father's weakening resolve, "I've also inherited your nose for a good story and if I can come up with one while I'm out there with the aid people, then TN will surely want to film it, won't they?"

"More than likely — if you do it well enough."

Julie laughed again. "You know I will. But I need your help, Dad."

"In what way?"

"I need to find a place on one of the aid convoys. I know Harry Green deals with that sort of coverage, so do you think he could help me get a place on one?"

"I'm having lunch with Harry — if that's any use," he said warily. "I suppose I could sound him out!"

"Thanks, Dad!" She brushed his

7

cheek with a grateful kiss.

"It's still dangerous . . . " Colin Stiller was feeling angry with himself now for giving in so easily.

"Dad, stop worrying! I'm not a kid any more! I know what I'm doing! Now, how about some coffee?"

"That must be the most sensible idea you've come up with all morning!"

As Julie disappeared into the kitchen, Stiller sat down in the chair and shivered slightly. The look on his face gave away what he was feeling.

Julie had been his whole life since his wife, Carol, had died. When they were just married, he had decided to take up Television North's offer to be their senior features editor. He had not regretted it.

Almost since the day she was born he, as a free-lance journalist, had dragged her and her mother around the globe on his varied assignments. But when they lost Carol to a sniper's bullet in South America, her death had hit them both hard. For Julie's sake, he had come home to Britain in the hope that, by doing so, it would ensure his daughter's chances of a new, safer, and more stable life.

He looked down at his hands. He knew he'd done his best for her but his conscience bothered him. He had spoiled his lovely daughter far too much and now, on top of everything else, she had clearly inherited his wandering bug, too. He knew what the trip to Moldova was about! She had made no secret of how much she was fascinated by her ancestors' blood-line. He had heard her with her friends, talking grandly of 'coming from old European stock', her innocence akin to the peasants of his father's land of birth. She would find a way to go back there, no matter what he said!

He grimaced slightly. Better that she went with his blessing. He knew there was nothing he could do now to stop her! She had to get it out of her system one way or the other!

Harry Green, a senior executive and principal shareholder of Television North, wiped his mouth with his napkin and leaned back in his chair. "So, where's the lovely Julie today, Colin?" he asked. "She wasn't in her office and I missed her. Is she OK?"

Stiller shook his head and pushed his empty plate to one side. "She's not ill, if that's what you're thinking."

"So, why do you look so worried?"

"I need a favour, Harry."

"You do? OK, so ask it."

"She wants to go to Moldova."

Harry nodded. "I know. She told me. And she told me, also, you are trying to talk her out of it."

Stiller shrugged. "Fat lot of good that's doing!"

Harry Green sighed, speaking very quietly. "Julie knows what she wants, Colin. And it could make a good story, have you thought of that? As a matter of fact, a convoy has been organised to go out to Rumania next week. It's a private charity, run by that German chap — "

"You mean, Bermann?"

"That's him. And the aid centre's somewhere near Timisoara, I believe — just a stone's throw from Moldova. Julie's pilgrimage to your family's old village is really no problem and would make excellent copy if it's handled in the right way."

"Mmm . . . "

Harry poured more wine, his pale eyes still on Stiller's face. "So, what's this favour you're after?"

Stiller replied wearily, his face hardening slightly, "If she does go — and it looks like she will — I want someone to go with her," adding hurriedly, "without her realising it, of course."

"Are you talking about some kind of bodyguard?"

Stiller shrugged. "Something like that — a guide perhaps. Someone who knows the area and can keep an eye on her. And I want a woman with her as well. I don't want my daughter traipsing off with just a group of men."

"Sure, sure, I understand." Harry's thick fingers unconsciously twirled the glass against the smooth surface of the table. Then he squinted up, surprise lighting the grey eyes as he glanced across the restaurant. "Well, well, just look who's here," he murmured.

"Who?" Stiller turned his head to see a balding, stocky man pull up a chair and sit down at a table near the door.

Harry went on, "That's who we've just been talking about — Dieter Bermann."

The two men nodded in Bermann's direction as he spotted them and, turning back, Harry resumed their conversation.

"So, where were we? Oh, yes, a bodyguard for Julie." He sighed, thinking a moment then speaking very quietly. "As coincidence would have it, only yesterday, we signed up someone for Rumania who's just the man to keep an eye on Julie for you."

"Who is it?"

"His name's Sometski — Jan Sometski. Polish chap. He works free-lance for us — speaks several languages. We use him as an interpreter as well as a reporter. We've used him a number of times for our Balkans coverage, and he's far and away the best."

"Jan Sometski . . . ?" Stiller looked uncertain. He had heard of him, of course, but had never actually met the man. He knew he was good, but he knew also that the man was a loner — a man who worked free-lance and refused to belong to any organisation or individual. He was good, but was he the man to whom he could trust his daughter?

"I don't know." Colin shook his head doubtfully.

"You say you want the best."

"I do, but — wasn't he involved in that Albanian fiasco?"

Harry Green smiled wryly. "Now you're letting rumour influence your better judgment."

"Fill me in on him, then."

Harry lit up a short cigar. "How much do you know of that Albania trip?"

Stiller shrugged unsurely. "Not much. I was still working abroad then and I only know that somebody got hurt."

"That's right." Harry tipped his head slightly in Dieter Bermann's direction. "It was one of his convoys as I remember, and if my memory serves me right, a girl that was on it died."

"What actually happened? I've forgotten the details."

"We had heard a rumour that there had been a build-up of arms into the Balkans," Harry told him, "and we wanted to find out who was supplying them so we sent Sometski on the same trip."

"So? What happened?"

"Well, there was trouble before they even started out. At first Sometski refused to go with only one supply truck and two Land-Rovers — he wanted protection."

"That's fair enough, knowing that part of the world."

Harry Green nodded. "We refused him all the same. We had no choice. The Albanian authorities insisted on a small party — one truck, two Land-Rovers — we were lucky to be allowed into the country at all!"

"What happened about the girl?"

Harry frowned, thoughtfully. "She was one of the aid workers — a nurse, I think — and it was said that she and Sometski had a sort of relationship." He looked upwards, thoughtfully, and shook his head, "I can't recall her name now . . . "

"It doesn't matter. What happened?"

"It seems there was trouble on the way back."

"What kind of trouble? With the girl?"

Harry Green shrugged, inhaling clouds of Havana tobacco. "There was an argument between Sometski and Bermann about her — Bermann tried to muscle in, as usual. Sometski warned him off, but Bermann forced her to travel in one of the Land-Rovers with him instead of in the truck with Sometski.

"It was January — a bad time to travel in the mountains, and there was a blizzard — a bad one! The conditions became almost impossible and it was Sometski who took over the task of getting them through. Anyway, on a narrow pass — well over three thousand metres up — they found the road had been blocked with snow and they had to dig their way through. It was then, Sometski told the Board of Enquiry later, that he realised Bermann's truck was missing — took a wrong turn, or something — and it was several hours before he managed to find him again . . . It wasn't until the next day, in fact, and when he did — "

"And when he did . . . ?"

"Sometski found Bermann wandering along the road alone, then sometime later he found the Land-Rover!"

"And the girl?"

"She wasn't in it. At the enquiry, Bermann insisted that she was behind him when he tried to find the road on foot but, somehow, I can't swallow that. Why leave the Land-Rover in the first place? Surely he must have known that the others would come looking for it! No, I believe there's more to it than just getting lost. I think he tried it on with her while he had the chance and she got scared. And then when she tried to get away from him she got hopelessly lost. It was a long time before they found her. She was about a mile from the Land-Rover, still on the mountain, frozen to death. And there had been signs of a struggle — "

"Oh, no!"

"The enquiry had no option but to call it death by misadventure." Harry Green shook his head again.

Stiller shook his head, his mouth bone dry. "And — if she'd been allowed to stay in the truck with the others she would still be alive," he commented quietly.

Harry Green sighed. "By the time Sometski finally found her, he was too late. He did his best to revive her — did everything he could! And he's never forgiven the German for that trip, I hear!" The big man laughed mirthlessly. "They say Sometski almost killed him when he finally got hold of him."

"I can't say I blame him."

For a moment neither man spoke then Colin, glancing at Harry Green sharply, muttered, "I don't fancy the idea of sending my Julie out there to risk freezing to death on a mountain."

"Sometski would never let that happen. If Julie insists on going on this trip she couldn't be with anyone better."

"How do you make that out?"

"Because, unlike Bermann, he knows the mountains well and he respects them! He wouldn't let Julie out of his sight!"

Stiller realised the sense of what Harry had just said but he still wasn't convinced. "Can he be trusted?"

Harry Green spread his hands. "He's the best."

"I mean with women. What's he like with women?"

"I've heard it said that's he's not interested any more. He prefers less emotional pursuits. Anyway, we pay him well and he wouldn't compromise his position with any fooling around. He does his job for us then," Harry Green lifted his hand and snapped his fingers in the air, "back he goes to his Highlands until the next time we send for him."

"Sounds a strange chap," Stiller commented wryly.

"He is! But he comes from a good family. Polish parents but with a dash of Scots from somewhere — even went to Oxford. He's a brilliant linguist. They say Sometski's real love is the land — he owns a place about twenty miles north of Invergordon." Harry Green helped himself to more wine.

"Can I trust him with my Julie?"

"You have my word."

Stiller considered. He sat still, head bent, his astute brain weighing up the odds. There was a long silence and then he said softly, "OK, Harry."

The big man nodded, grinning. "I'll get on to it right away."

The two men rose from the table and shook hands. Harry Green went up to the desk and handed over a credit card while Colin Stiller waited for him by the door. Dieter Bermann looked up from his food, his mouth full and his head nodding his acknowledgement as they passed his table.

"Hello, Dieter," Harry said to him.

Bermann swallowed quickly. "Harry! Nice to see you again."

"This is Colin Stiller."

Stiller shook the German's hand, noticing the man's plate piled with food.

"I'd like a word this afternoon, Dieter, if you're free."

"Sure! Sure! Any time. Is it about my trip?"

Harry nodded briefly. "Yes, as a matter of fact it is. Colin's daughter, Julie, wants to go out to Rumania to make a film. We wondered if you could fix it for her to join your group next week?"

"I'll see what I can do."

"Better make the arrangements for two, Dieter. I want Sometski to go with you as well."

Dieter Bermann's head jerked up. "Sometski?"

"That's right. Anyway, I'll talk it over with you later, OK?"

The two men turned and left the restaurant. If they had looked back to see Dieter Bermann's expression, they might even have felt a little sorry for him. He turned abruptly back to his food, all enjoyment for it gone.

Jan Sometski! Would he never get from under his skin?

2

JAN SOMETSKI was reasonably pleased with the way the meeting had gone. He was even more pleased to get out of the over-heated office. And, as he drove off the car park and waited for a break in the traffic, he looked back at the huge steel and glass complex that made up the offices of Television North.

Moving off, Jan Sometski pushed on the radio button and thought about the girl. She was to join him next week in Budapest, on the way to Rumania. They had told him that, apart from her voluntary assistance with the aid work, she would be spending a couple of days in Moldova to do some filming and it was his job to see that she came to no harm.

He sighed. It would be no picnic! Didn't they realise just how dangerous the Balkans could be these days? And it puzzled him that they were sending an inexperienced girl to do the filming in the first place, but, on the other hand, he wasn't complaining. They'd met his escort fee without a word. He'd take her to Moldova if that's what she wanted! All the same, she'd be far better off staying put — safe and sound within the centrally-heated environment of her comfortable Yorkshire home.

He moved on through the traffic, threading his way along the one-way system until he reached the turn-off that would take him to his flat. At the junction, he stopped for the lights and watched a group of German journalists stroll out of a bar. He recognised most of them. They had been part of the team on his last trip to Berlin. What a waste of time that had proved to be! He had spent over a month trying to cover the momentous breaching of the wall but, coming from the East, all they'd really wanted was a taste of West Berlin's night spots.

Jan Sometski glanced at the digital clockface on the dashboard as he turned into his drive. Oonie would have gone home by now. As always, his flat would be clean and his evening meal prepared. And, in spite of what people thought, the girl and he weren't a couple. Since he had lost Anna — and had been sickened by Helga — he had had no lasting relationship with any girl. As he turned his key in the door, he wondered if he ever would again. He doubted it.

He opened the door then paused, his body tensing instinctively. Something was not quite right. A lamp still shone from the sitting-room and he walked silently towards it, pushing open the door.

But Jan Sometski relaxed as the shy, round face of the Filipino girl turned to him as he went warily through. "Oonie!" he said. "What are you doing here at this time? You should be home by now."

"Mister Jan!" Oonie's face had

24

lost its usual calm and she looked frightened. "Mister Jan, you — you have a visitor."

He sighed and glanced at his watch. "Who?"

"He would not give his name, and he would not leave."

"I thought I told you never to let anyone in when I am away."

The girl nodded, shame-faced, and Jan Sometski sighed again.

"Never mind, Oonie. Where is he now?"

The girl pointed to the balcony. "Out there."

"Right, I'll see him. Now, you must go home. Your family will worry."

The girl nodded again, murmuring her apologies as she fled from the room. Jan Sometski frowned towards the balcony, wondering who could be waiting to see him this late in the day. He was tired. He didn't need any company tonight and he was sensing an atmosphere that he didn't like.

For a few moments, he didn't move.

Then he took a step forward, stopping abruptly as his visitor emerged from the shadows.

"You!" Jan's tone was without expression.

The visitor stepped forward, the silence between the two men continuing for perhaps thirty seconds.

Dieter Bermann had worked out what he would say on the way here but, now that he faced Jan Sometski, he suddenly wanted a drink, conscious of the sweat along his upper lip.

He asked his question in German. "You're escorting a girl to Uj-Moldova?" And when Jan gave a curt nod of his head, Dieter continued, "It is with my team that you are to travel, did you know that?"

"So Green has informed me!" The tone was scathing and Jan made no attempt to disguise his hatred. "What about it? Why have you come here?" Just to see the man under his roof was making him sick. "Don't tell me she's something to do with you?" He hurled his words at the man.

"Have you accepted the commission?"

"I have!"

The German's smile was mocking. "In spite of the fact that we will be travelling together again?"

Jan stared at the man for several seconds before almost spitting out his next words. "I signed the contract before they told me it was you who would be leading it!"

Bermann's smile widened. "Perhaps they believe the girl will be safer with me there as well. Perhaps they don't trust you enough to leave her solely in your hands. Anyway, I'm sure Helga will not like the girl so much, especially knowing how she felt about you in Albania."

"Helga? You're taking Helga?"

"They want the girl to have a chaperon, so who else would I choose but Helga?"

That was enough for Jan Sometski. He turned away abruptly, brushing the man aside to stand by the balcony's open door. "Helga is your girl! Now, if that's all you have to say, get out of here, Bermann!"

"Better look after this Stiller girl, Jan," Dieter went on with quiet mockery. "We wouldn't want anything to happen to her through your carelessness, would we?"

Jan looked out into the darkness, barely keeping his temper. Presently, he turned back, voicing his contempt. "You say that after what you did to Anna?" His tone was hostile. "Do you remember, Bermann? How she looked? How you stood there — on that mountain road — trembling like a child?" Jan shuddered, holding on to his reason as he relived the moment.

Slowly, he went on, "You're taking a chance coming here tonight. And whoever the girl is, I pity her if she gets mixed up with you."

The German backed away as Jan stepped nearer — he had sampled the anger of Sometski before. "I'll take as much care of her as I would anyone in my team." Jan laughed coldly. "I can't say that your coming here tonight has endeared her to me, but she'll be in better hands than Anna was. Now, get out of here before I break your neck."

Dieter Bermann needed no second telling. He cleared his throat. "I just needed to let you know," was all he could say and then he left the room quickly.

Jan lifted his eyes to the night sky, forcing his mind into limbo. Would he ever come to terms with Anna's death? He stood silently, the thermostat of the air-conditioning clicking softly, and the breeze from it wafting the blue-striped curtains at the windows. There was a small sound behind him and something touched his arm. He sprang around, as though awakened from an uneasy sleep. "What the — "

The girl started, terrified by the look on his face. "I go now, Mister Jan. Your supper is ready."

Jan Sometski sighed, the anger

leaving his face, "I'm sorry, Oonie, I didn't mean to frighten you." He looked down into the girl's gentle dark eyes. "It's very late. You know how much your family worries."

She smiled and turned away, anxious now to get home to her family. "Goodnight, Mister Jan."

When the girl had gone, Jan showered and ate his supper and then went to lie on his bed. He ran his hands through his thick, dark hair and then pressed the heels of them against the high, Slavic, cheek-bones of his face. He thought of the girl he would be meeting in Budapest, and of their journey from Rumania to Moldova.

Jan gathered himself and reached over to take a set of maps from his bedside drawer, flipping them over and looking up the route he must decide would be the safest.

The girl's destination was to be Uj-Moldova — a small town in the Banat that had lain forgotten by the world for over seventy years. It was an odd place

30

for anyone to want to film.

Recently annexed to Russia, it was now independent and lay snuggled below the southern slopes of the Carpathian mountains. He had heard of some trouble there last year — a flare-up between the hardline rebels and the fledgling Moldovan militia. But it seemed quiet enough now. After a bloody six months or so, the ceasefire seemed to be holding out. He studied the map for a few minutes more and then he yawned, flicking off the light and falling into a deep sleep.

★ ★ ★

Sometski's first glimpse of Julie Stiller was as she stepped off the aircraft that had brought her to Budapest. Her hair was blonde and she moved easily, a shoulder-bag slung across her shoulder. She was smiling, putting out her hand and, when she spoke, her voice was low and warm and without a trace of affectation.

"Jan Sometski? I'm Julie Stiller."

"Miss Stiller."

The girl's blue eyes looked around. "So, here we are then!"

"I sincerely hope so, Miss Stiller, since I assume this was your destination."

Julie looked up sharply, catching the ironic humour of his tone before answering him drily. "They didn't prepare me for your sense of humour."

He didn't answer and, for a wary moment, the two sized each other up. She was curious about the man who had been assigned to accompany her on the most interesting journey of her life and, from the look on his face, she was clearly not what he had been expecting! But then, he wasn't what she'd imagined him to be either!

She laughed softly. "What's the matter, Mr Sometski? You look surprised!"

Jan frowned, thinking he hadn't seen such blue eyes smile at him like this for a long, long time. Then he shrugged. "Not much surprises me, Miss Stiller. Come on, I will drive you to our hotel.

The film crew are already there, but the drivers and the medics are at the 'Erzebet'. We will meet up with them tomorrow."

"Fine."

He led her towards a car and, as they left the airport to take the thirty minute drive into the centre of Budapest, Jan gave a brief outline of the schedule.

In all, there were to be fifteen lorries on the trip, sent from various charities and stacked with all the necessary blankets, food, clothing and medical supplies. She would be in his own small party of three cars.

In the first one, besides herself and Jan, would be the German, Dieter and his girlfriend, Helga. The second car would carry the two TV engineers and their recording paraphanalia, and, finally, in the third car would be the small group of medical volunteers.

Julie mentally filed all this information in interested silence, and only spoke when Jan Sometski suggested that the German nurse, Helga Bauer, would also act as her chaperon.

"Who says I need a chaperon?" she asked, turning to him in evident surprise. "Was it your idea?"

Sometski shook his head, smiling grimly. "Not guilty!" he said. "Apparently, when TN saw her name on the list of volunteers, someone thought it might be a good idea to keep you two females together."

Julie sighed resignedly. "My father!"

Jan shrugged. "I've no idea."

"But it's ridiculous!"

"I agree. And Helga wouldn't be my choice for anyone's chaperon, but she's the only other female in the party."

Julie gave him a quick, sideways glance, picking up something in his tone. "Do you know her?"

"I'm afraid I do."

By now, they had reached the city and, in the late afternoon's light, Julie had her first view of the Danube. Her eyes swept along its graceful curve, looking over to the old town of Buda and at the tracery of bridges that bound it to its twin city, Pest. It was beautiful, elegant, and charming. It was all of those things but, disappointingly, it was not at all blue!

When they got to the hotel they went over to the desk to register and, as they waited for the receptionist to wade through the piles of red tape, a man broke away from a group of people sitting at a bar and stepped forward to greet them. He was large and overweight, and his slightly bloated face was already weighing up the undoubted charms of Julie Stiller, his grey eyes narrowed in interested speculation.

"Welcome to Budapest, Miss Stiller," he said as she shook his hand. "Allow me to introduce myself. My name is Dieter Bermann. Come, meet the others. Jan can handle all the paperwork here — he's used to it." And before she could say a word, Dieter Bermann led her over to the bar to introduce her to the rest of the group.

As Julie shook their hands she weighed up her new travelling companions.

There was Jack, the cameraman and Ben, the sound engineer, both amiable and intelligent, and with that slightly world-weary manner that seems to be a necessary trademark with people in the media.

Rather unmannerly by leaving her until the last, Dieter finally introduced her to the German nurse. "Julie, this is Helga Bauer, she's the one to call upon if you ever need an aspirin."

The girl shook Julie's proffered hand, but did not return her smile. She sat silent and stiff upon the bar stool, her left hand fingering the fine gold locket that was around her neck, the single letter H intertwined inside a heart. And it was only when Jan Sometski joined them a few moments later that the girl's head lifted and her two wide, suggestive eyes rested eagerly upon his face.

Julie's quick mind summed up the situation between Helga Bauer and Jan Sometski right away. The woman was in love with him! And, Julie conceded, who could blame her? Jan Sometski was an attractive man — she had felt his sensuality for herself the moment his hand had touched hers at the airport.

After the introductory drinks and a modicum of small talk, the party then dispersed to their rooms to prepare for their journey next day. And, as she looked around her own — the room she was forced to share with Helga — she decided it was plain, but functional. There were no luxuries and Julie expected none.

"Which bed do you prefer, Helga?" she asked once they were alone.

Her question was answered by a shrug and a heavily-accented, "I don't care."

Julie had already got the message. If she'd hoped to make a friend of Helga Bauer, then she might as well forget it.

She threw her case on the bed by the door, unpacked her nightwear and a change of clothes for tomorrow and took off her dress. Then, wrapping herself in a robe, she went out along the passage, stepping gingerly along the creaking floorboards until she found the bathroom. Then, a little while later, clean and refreshed, Julie went back into the bedroom to find the other girl seated in a cane chair by the dressing-table and polishing her nails.

She made another attempt at conversation.

"The bathroom's an experience, Helga," she said, keeping her tone light. "Have you tried it?"

The girl shrugged. "I bathed this morning." She looked up, the wide-spaced eyes glittering their hostility.

Ignoring it, Julie persisted in her efforts. "Is this your first trip with an aid convoy?"

"To Rumania, yes! But Jan and I are old friends, you understand? We have worked together before."

"I see. Where was that?"

"Oh here and there . . . " She shot Julie a ferocious glance as she added, "You understand? Jan is my friend."

Julie let out a short, surprised laugh. "Are you trying to warn me off?"

"If you like," Helga Bauer raised a hand dismissively. "Jan and I have an — an understanding. Perhaps if you have ideas for yourself, you had better ask him about us. I'm sure he will be only too pleased to enlighten you."

Julie Stiller gave another small laugh. "Perhaps I would, if I was interested enough."

Helga shrugged dismissively as she got up and crossed over to her bed to lie down. Her movement was graceful and, even though Julie already had enough reason to dislike the woman, she had to admit to her striking good looks.

The two girls didn't speak again. Julie lay down on her own bed and began to wonder what on earth she'd let herself in for.

Then, the plane journey and the fatigue of the last few days began to take their toll and soon, Julie became a little drowsy. She had almost fallen asleep when a knock on the door roused her. It opened briefly to reveal the head of Jan Sometski.

"Better get dressed. We're meeting downstairs in two minutes."

Julie raised her head from the pillow. "What? Now?"

"Yes."

"Me, too?"

"Of course, you too. That's if you still want to go into Rumania!" He nodded towards Helga's slumbering form. "It doesn't matter about Helga. She knows the routine. Leave her here. Let her finish her beauty sleep."

Julie dressed quickly and, when she went downstairs a few minutes later, Jack, Ben and Dieter Bermann were already seated on an old, leather couch that had seen far better days. The German beckoned her over and patted the couch, "Here, Julie, sit by me. Drink?"

"Yes, please. I'll try some wine. What's this meeting all about?"

"It's a ritual." The German laughed

fatuously and called for a bottle of the local wine, then added, Julie thought, rather bitterly, "Jan always likes us to know what we're up against."

Jan Sometski dragged a chair across and sat down. He pulled a table between them and unrolled a map. He examined it, then, finding the place he wanted, stabbed a finger down and, for the first time, Julie noticed the gold bracelet around his muscular wrist, and the Polish eagle that had been engraved upon it.

"This is where we can expect some trouble," he warned them.

The German yawned and mopped his face with a handkerchief. He didn't seem the least interested in the route into Rumania, but Julie was intrigued.

Jan Sometski indicated to a point on the map and continued, "This is the way we must go, it's the safest."

"What's the worst danger?" she asked, leaning forward to see better.

"The whole place is dangerous," Jan Sometski answered wryly as she turned her face to look across at him. He smiled for the first time and she was quite surprised at its gentleness. A brief silence stretched between them and he stared at her now with the blank look of a man on the defensive. "There's still time to turn back," he said at last. "There will be nights when our only accommodation will be a tent and a sleeping bag. Would that bother you?"

Julie smiled, her sense of humour rising. "Of course not! I was a good Girl Guide."

He turned abruptly, reverting his attention to the map. "Very well. We'll have to leave the main route here." He circled a point with his finger. "After that, we continue on to Senta by this road until we reach our first relief centre . . . " Jan Sometski paused, throwing her a brief glance. "The roads are poor up there, it won't be very comfortable."

"I never expected it to be," she answered immediately.

"What he means, Julie," Jack put in, "is that Rumania isn't exactly a pleasant drive along a pleasant, English lane."

"I know what he means." She glanced back at Jan. "But what kind of trouble can we expect?"

Jan Sometski shrugged. "Perhaps none," he murmured, "but we must be on our guard. There are too many rebels roaming the mountains for my liking — teenagers, mostly — who would quite willingly steal our trucks. They're fanatics! They'd kill for our petrol and our supplies — the black market pays them well."

Jan slanted her a look, his expression briefly registering an interested curiosity before he smiled and turned away again.

Dieter Bermann had followed the glance and marked it. Perhaps the old Sometski magic was working again. He reached into the pocket of his leather jacket, taking out a cigar case and selecting one. He lit up and stuck it into the side of his mouth, staring moodily into space, locking and interlocking his soft white fingers.

"We go tomorrow," Sometski concluded, folding the map and getting to his feet. "Tonight, I suggest you get plenty of sleep. It will be the last decent bed you will lie on for many a night."

A little while later, when Julie went back up to her room, she found Helga still fast asleep. She stepped out on to the veranda that ran along the length of the hotel, breathing in the night air and moving away from the room's dim light.

Then a sound crept into her consciousness. She felt a shadowy figure lean against the rail beside her and she turned her head to see who it was, peering hard into the darkness.

"They say that nothing quite compares to the stars over the Blue Danube," Jan Sometski's deep voice came softly.

Julie glanced upwards. Above them the vast, dark sky was silent. "It does look very beautiful."

"But, beautiful as this night is, Miss Stiller, it would be better that you sleep. Tomorrow will be hard."

She glanced up and her eyes met his. The fickle moon was lighting his face and, for one brief moment, the world faded. A shudder ran through her. There was something about those eyes . . .

"Good-night, Miss Stiller."

Julie swallowed. "Good-night."

She moved away and walked back towards her room, still feeling his eyes burning into her back as she closed the door behind her.

3

JAN SOMETSKI woke early, yawned, stretched, then turned to look at the German still snoring in the bed beside him.

"Come on, get up!" Jan shook him. "It's turned six and we've a long way to go today."

Dieter Bermann blinked open a puffy eye before turning on his back and rubbing his eyes with the tips of his soft, white fingers. "What time did you say it was?" he grunted.

"Time we made a move. We need to be at least half-way to the border by nightfall."

"We'll make it. This trip's important to me, too, you know. After all, I've funded two of the lorries myself."

He turned over again and Jan frowned. He pulled on his clothes and moved to the window, throwing back the shutters. The daylight blazed in, making him blink. He was still tired. He hadn't slept as well as he normally did and he knew the reason why.

Mentally, he thrust the Stiller girl out of his thoughts and concentrated on the trip ahead, unlatching the glass door and stepping out on to the ornate wrought-iron balcony to look down at the activity in the street below.

Most of the convoy had already drawn up outside the hotel and some of the drivers were checking out the tyres and the lights. Leaving Bermann where he was, Jan went downstairs.

Jan swallowed a cup of coffee and then, for the hundredth time, checked out the party's travel permits before going outside and thrusting them into a leather satchel that was stowed behind the back seat of the car. Then, once he'd given Jack and Ben a hand with the TV gear, he climbed in the front and sat moodily at the wheel.

He glanced up as Julie's slim form appeared in the hotel doorway, and he watched her as she came down the steps and made her way towards the car. Jan cursed inwardly, conscious that her movements were graceful even at this early hour in the day. Somewhere in his gut, a long-stilled ache intensified, deepening even more so as she smiled at him through the car's wound-down window, a canvas hold-all hooked over her shoulder.

She had covered her blonde hair back with a scarf, and the grey, denim trousers and faded, green, bomber-jacket were practical. But the trousers also hugged the tops of her long legs — giving Jan ideas he hadn't had for a long time and he turned quickly away, occupying himself with the windscreen-wiper switch.

Julie got in beside him, greeting him with a bright smile and an air of exuberant freshness. But, as she chatted on, he found he wasn't really listening. He could smell her scent, and he was far too conscious of the hot feeling that had settled in his body. Concentration was difficult as he fiddled with the switch, and then, turning to look at her animated face, Jan began to wonder about Julie Stiller.

Dieter Bermann's sleep-thickened voice broke into his thoughts, "I thought you were in a rush! How long before we go?"

Jan glared out at the German. "Five minutes, with any luck! What's keeping Helga?"

Bermann shrugged, shook his head and shuffled off towards one of the drivers. Watching him, Jan wished he wasn't coming — or his girlfriend! He neither liked nor trusted either of the Germans, but the man had organised it all so there wasn't very much he could do. Besides, Dieter Bermann had contacts and they might come in useful and where Dieter went, so did Helga! He would have to put up with their devious ways for a few weeks more and hoped it would be worth it.

He excused himself as he swung his long frame out of the car, and, feeling less than useless, Julie climbed out of the car, too. She had to do something! Besides, the action helped to bring her back to reality, her brain unwilling to admit the momentary weakness she was beginning to feel whenever Jan Sometski was near. She could feel, even now, how close he was, but she didn't care to look at him again — not until she had her wayward feelings back under firm control.

Helga made her appearance some fifteen minutes later. And, Julie thought, taking in the short, tight skirt and the white blouse, she looked more equipped for a day at the office than the long hard trek they were taking on. When they were all finally ready to leave, the good-looking German girl wriggled herself into the car's passenger seat, marking her place next to Jan.

Sometski threw Julie a quick, searching glance. He had thought this might happen and wondered if Julie would complain. After all, her father was paying his fee and, he reasoned, she had the right to demand the most comfort, but Julie made no complaint. She returned his glance with a brief, perceptive stare and turned away quickly, climbing into the back seat with Dieter Bermann.

Jan admired her composure, but didn't fancy the idea of her stuck in the back with the German for the long hours before they reached the forest clearing at Kistelek — the place he had chosen for their over-night stop.

"Just a temporary arrangement," he mumbled as he got in beside Helga. "I'll see you get the comfort of the front seat soon!"

"Don't worry about me, I'm all right."

But, as they started off, Julie wondered if perhaps that was too optimistic a remark.

Following the procession of lorries, they headed east towards the Rumanian border. Once out of the capital, the road became less smooth, and around them Julie could see the huddled villages and the high-looming outline of the mountains.

Apart from a couple of brief stops for lunch, eight, uncomfortable hours passed before they finally reached their over-night destination. After braking suddenly and negotiating two miles or so of dense thicket and spruce they turned into a clearing. Judging from the small scattering of empty cola and beer cans, and the abandoned wreck of an old Volkswagen, the clearing obviously acted as a sort of camp site for any itinerant passer-by. It was unseen from the road, tucked away off a side-track and, untidy or not, the place was like paradise to Julie Stiller. She felt she'd been travelling for ever but, when she glanced at the mileage dial, they'd only covered three hundred miles.

"We'll camp here tonight," Jan told them. "We'll cross the border tomorrow."

With great relief Julie climbed out, moving carefully so as not to awaken the sleeping Dieter. Once out of the car, she breathed in deeply, taking long, gulping breaths of the pine-scented air. She felt hot and sticky and would have given her right arm for a shower just then. Taking a few steps forward Julie paused, already wilted by the strength-sapping atmosphere of the cramped back-seat journey.

"You look tired." Jan Sometski glanced at her as she leaned against the car, giving her one of his rare smiles. "And this is only the beginning. Are you OK?"

Julie grinned ruefully, "I'm sore."

Jan smiled again. "You'll get used to it."

Julie switched on her video camera and started on her first reel of film, covering the group as they unpacked and prepared their first hot meal of the day.

Helga was still sitting lazily in the car with the door flung open, and swiping at an insect that had settled on her skirt — a skirt which was now hitched high above her knees.

Jan Sometski glowered. "Cover up, Helga," was his gruff advice, glancing warily at the other drivers. "This is no pool side and you ought to know better."

The girl's full lips curved into a smile that didn't quite reach her eyes. "Does it bother you, darling," she chafed teasingly, adding as she lowered her eyes towards the group of men.

Jan merely glared, contempt for the girl showing clearly in his dark eyes, and the German girl shrugged and turned away.

Dieter Bermann, awake at last, stood a little apart from the rest and puffed at a cigar. He was watching everything, his face white and his lips drawn into a tight line. Then he got up and positioned himself beside Helga and muttered something to her in German, the words unintelligible to Julie's English ear.

Jan strode away and Julie, still ostensibly filming the camp site, watched fascinated as the two Germans talked quietly together. Helga had turned her attention to Dieter now and was stroking a placating hand along his cheek. Julie knew exactly what Helga was about. The girl was a manipulator!

"Fancy a bite?" With a little start, Julie turned quickly as Ben handed her plate. "It's not exactly the Savoy Grill." He grinned. "But it's nice and hot."

Thanking him, Julie put aside the camera and took the dish, giving a wary glance at the lurid-looking stew. She grimaced inwardly. It didn't look at all appetising but she was hungry enough to eat anything. So, after finding herself a canvas stool, she tucked in to the thick, dark, paprika-flavoured broth and found it most delicious.

In spite of the good, nourishing meal, it was a sombre party that shared the supper and very little was said. Everyone seemed tired — everyone, that is except Jan, who despite the long, hot day and the humid, night air, seemed unflagging in his constant attention to detail. And, later, when a passing group of inquisitive, local militia demanded to see their papers, he handled them all with polite, yet dignified, composure.

After supper, the drivers settled down for the night in their cabs while the rest of them put up their tents. And, when they had finished, Julie was by now so tired that she ached. Her bones still hurt from the miles on the jolting roads, and, momentarily, she thought longingly of her home in York and of her cooling shower and the soft, white towels and her comfortable bed that would be unoccupied tonight.

She smiled wryly. She hoped it wasn't to be a case of the spirit was willing, but the flesh was weak because this was only the beginning! There would be no comfortable beds for weeks. Well, she'd asked for it, hadn't she? But, looking at the little circle of glum faces around her, she had rather hoped for more lively company.

Later, squeezing herself into the tent

she was to share with Helga and unzipping her sleeping bag, Julie once more felt that small stab of excitement nip around her gut and, as she checked the video cassette inside the camera, she wondered what tomorrow would bring.

With a little laugh, she took off her top clothes and slipped into the sleeping bag, glancing subconsciously at the luminous dial of her watch. It was almost midnight! Then, turning on her side, she peered out of the slit of an opening, watching Jan Sometski as he paced around the clearing — a tall, lonely figure, a gun at his side.

★ ★ ★

Jan opened his eyes, drowsy, still half asleep, his limbs cramped by the narrowness of the sleeping bag. He had been dreaming of a girl. He thought at first it had been Anna because her hand was warm and silky and tanned as it stroked against his face. It took him a moment to realise he wasn't dreaming at all! There was someone in the tent with him! He felt the soft hand press against his hair and, when he lifted his face to look, the eyes that looked back were no brown and smiling dream, they were real — grey, wide-spaced, and calculating.

He edged himself up, sudden premonition jerking him awake as the soft, German voice came again. "Why do you avoid me so, Jan?"

He stood up, putting a good three feet of space between them and advised quietly, "Would you just get out of here, Helga."

Helga Bauer's expression held the look of a small, hungry animal. "But I've seen how you look at me," she whispered. "How I make you feel . . . "

"You don't make me feel anything! Not you! I suggest you go back to Dieter!"

Helga took a step towards him, her lovely face pale in the moonlight. "I don't want Dieter — you know I don't." Then before he could move, Helga had flung herself forward, her whole being alight with excitement as she grasped her arms around his neck and held him tight. "You know I don't want Dieter . . . "

Jan backed away, grabbing her arms and forcing them from his neck. "Get out of here — "

He flung open the flap and strode outside the tent, but Helga was right behind him, and now Jan could feel her trembling as she threw her arms around him again.

His own arms came up abruptly, clamping on hers with a force like steel and dragging them down. "What's the matter with you? Don't you know you'll wake the others?"

"I don't care! I don't care anything for the others."

Jan Sometski stared at the girl blankly. What did it take to get rid of her? "It's over! Go back to your tent and stay there!"

59

Helga Bauer reached up, trying to embrace him again but this time he was ready. His hands, broad-backed and powerful, were upon her and thrusting her away. "Go away, Helga."

He turned away, abandoning his tent and striding towards the car, and leaving the German girl shaking with outrage and humiliation.

Julie had awakened with a start. She wondered for a moment where she was then, remembering, she glanced again at her watch. It was still only two o'clock. Her eyes flicked across the tent, expecting to see Helga lying there, but the sleeping bag was empty.

She turned on to her back, listening. Sounds had disturbed her. As her ears became accustomed, she recognised the voices of Jan Sometski and Helga Bauer.

A sudden, sharp tear of disappointment dragged at her as, surreptitiously, she looked out of the flap again. The moon was full — as bright as day — and, standing less than a hundred yards away, was Jan and Helga was folded into his arms.

Julie turned back again quickly. After all, their affair was nothing to do with her! The German girl's beauty was enough to tempt a saint, let alone a man like Sometski.

Julie felt more than disappointment. She hadn't had him down as that kind of man. Was he that kind of man? Was that why her father had been so against her coming on this trip?

She lay staring at the tent's ceiling, her arms locked above her head. She wondered about Jan Sometski. How could he treat a girl so callously? And what kind of a woman would allow it? She wondered too, why the thought of them together was making her feel so sad!

At first light next morning, they breakfasted on bread rolls and fruit. And, once they were under way again, Julie stared out at the uncomfortable miles ahead.

"How long will it take us to reach

the refugee centre?" she asked no-one in particular.

"Four, maybe five hours or so," Sometski replied. "But we should be at the border in another two hours. Let's hope the guards don't present too many problems."

Julie glanced at him, "Do you think they might?"

"I doubt it!" Dieter said. "A handful of marks is usually enough to stop any trouble."

She threw another glance at Jan. "Bribery?"

He grinned, answering calmly. "They expect it — it's a way of life. Their money is useless, so foreign currency opens many doors." His grin widened. "Don't worry about it."

He sounded confident enough and, resolutely, she turned her eyes away. He had a nice grin. It was a pity he didn't smile more often. She sighed inwardly, wondering what she could do about her fascination with the man. His face was taut in the brightness of the sun's light but he seemed less tense this morning. There was even a light-hearted flippancy in his tone as he added, "Will you pass me the bottle of water?"

She reached for the bottle from the pocket of the door, unscrewing the cap and handing it to him. As he pressed it to his lips to take a long swig, Julie thought silently that if there was a flaw in his features at all, it was perhaps that his chin was a little too cleft.

Julie sat back in the passenger seat and closed her eyes. In spite of the fans blowing from the dashboard and the windows wound right down, the temperature was already climbing. From behind she could hear the sound of voices speaking in German — Helga's shrill and impatient, Dieter's deep and amused.

Jan had insisted that Julie take the front seat today and it sounded — judging from the sharp note of petulance in her tone — as though Helga was still complaining about it.

She glanced at her watch. They must, by now, have covered more than sixty miles and she looked out at the beautiful countryside around them, and then upwards at the speck of a plane.

For almost an hour no-one spoke and then, as the road widened and the lorry in front of them slowed down, its brake lights glowing amber, Jan informed her, "We're almost at the border now." He half-turned to Dieter and added quietly, "Better get the papers ready — we don't want to waste too much time."

The convoy approached the border posts. They had made good time. And as two grey-uniformed guards stepped out of their hut, Julie could hear their light-hearted banter with the drivers. If the Rumanian guards were in as good a mood as the Hungarians seemed to be, she mused, the formalities would be quickly over.

One of the guards walked slowly towards the car and he called out something that Julie could not understand.

Dieter called back, and handed over the satchel that contained their papers. And, after a few moments perusal, he waved them on towards the frontier barrier.

Julie reached for her camera. This was a shot too good to miss.

"Put that away!" Jan snapped urgently, pushing the video camera out of sight. "These guys seem friendly enough, but they can be very sensitive about having their photographs taken."

Slowly, they travelled the few hundred yards of No-Man's Land that separated Hungary from Rumania. The guards there, too, it seemed, were in no mood for work and, when Dieter leaned out of the window to call out to one of them, a tall, bearded soldier in an ill-fitting uniform ambled over slowly.

Dieter mumbled in his ear and slipped something into his hand and the man looked down to inspect it. A second guard appeared, muttering impatiently to his colleague before turning to Dieter in an angry, complaining manner. And then, within minutes — and to Julie's dismay — the three of them began to argue. As the row began to turn more sinister, Julie grew more anxious by the minute until, cursing audibly, Dieter produced more inducement from his wallet and the two men seemed finally satisfied.

They pocketed the money and strolled towards the trucks, making a long, drawn-out inspection of them until, to Julie's great sigh of relief, they waved the convoy on.

Two hours later, they were crossing the Tiszas river and, by mid-afternoon, had reached the aid centre eight miles north of Varchovina.

The centre had once been a convent, a large, long, house that had been built inside a hill. A glass-covered veranda ran along the front of it, with seats the nuns once used in their solitary moments of leisure time. Today, those seats held the waiting aid workers — village people, and mainly women. When they went inside, Julie found the entrance bare and stark with nothing but a long table that was placed by the door to receive their precious aid.

"Will they bother if I film the unloading?" Julie asked, reaching hesitantly for the video camera.

"I doubt it!" Jan's dark eyes glittered as he observed the head-scarfed huddle of women and murmured, "I should think they're getting used to it by now."

Julie switched on her camera and wandered amongst the group, smiling encouragingly into the inquisitive faces of the women. She noticed that, of the men remaining in the village, most were old. The younger ones, Jan explained, would be off into the cities to work — or into the militia.

A little later, when she'd packed the camera away, Jan led her towards a pale, quiet-looking woman who stood apart from the rest.

"Come on," he said, "I'll introduce you to Frau Sedlacek. She runs the place."

Jan spoke fluently in the local dialect to the pale-faced woman. It was hard to tell her age, but Julie put her somewhere between forty or fifty. Once the ritual of greeting was done, the courteous and kindly woman led them through to a room at the end of the hallway and opened the door, gesturing for Julie to step inside.

"They save this room for their guests," Jan explained, adding ruefully as Julie's eyes swept around the cold, barely furnished dormitory, "I agree, it's nothing to write home about, but at least it's clean." He appraised her upturned face. "Anyway, dump your things in it and then we'll go over and pay respects to the man in charge."

"I don't suppose there's any chance of a shower?" Julie asked, not fancying the idea of meeting anyone in her hot and sticky state.

Jan followed her glance towards another room along the passage. Its door had been left slightly ajar and it was revealing an old-fashioned iron bath.

"Don't expect the Ritz." He grinned. "But I'll see what I can do. What mains there are here are erratic, so the water supply is a bit hit or miss."

"I see."

With a small, resigned shrug, Julie went back outside again to collect her canvas bag, and a few minutes later when she returned to the stiflingly shuttered dormitory, she found Helga already there, staking her claim to the most comfortable of the two made-up sleeping cots.

Julie thought silently as she watched her, what a pity it was that the girl could not suppress her dislike of her. She had noticed, too, that since last night, she and Jan — especially Jan — had hardly passed a word.

When Julie went back outside again several minutes later, Dieter was directing the unloading of the aid crates, concentrating mainly on the two trucks which, he informed her, he had supplied

69

himself. As she walked back down the steps to help, she suddenly felt a small tug at her jeans and she glanced down.

A Rumanian boy — no more than four or five — was looking up, a bright, friendly smile on his small, grubby face and one of the charity's knitted toys gripped tightly in his hand.

Julie greeted him in English. "Hello!"

"Hello!" The boy giggled and prodded his thin chest with a finger. "Me . . . Karol . . . "

She bent down to shake his tiny hand. "Well, Karol, I'm very pleased to meet you."

"Don't get too friendly with them," she heard Helga warn sullenly from behind her. "They're always after something and, if they think you're a soft touch, they'll never leave you alone."

"I'll try to remember that," Julie replied coldly.

Back in the convent, after helping to unload the stacks of blankets, food, and medical aid, and filming more of the activity as she did so, Julie tidied herself as best she could, wiping away the sticky grime with her sponge and combing her hair back from her face. Later, she followed Helga into what was once the refectory where a simple meal had been laid. As she entered, the little boy, Karol, ran forward and clung on to her hand.

"Who's your friend?" Jan asked, casting a wary eye at the boy.

"He says his name is Karol."

The boy smiled up at her with his great, brown eyes.

"Better not get too friendly with him," Jan warned her.

"Why not?"

"Most of these children are trained to beg."

He spoke rapidly to the boy in his own language and the child broke away, turning to run back to the group of women who were working in the kitchen. Then Jan smiled inwardly as Julie threw him a stony look and called the boy back again. He should have known she would like kids. How different the two women were. He could not imagine Helga taking such an interest.

After supper, they walked across the village square towards another house where a tall man was waiting by the door to greet them. By his side was a younger version of himself and, as they entered, Julie felt Karol's hand creep into her own.

Franz Jantner stepped forward to greet them.

"Welcome!" he said in English, his voice deep and his smile slow. "My son and I bid you welcome."

He added something else in his own language which Julie did not understand and Jan responded, turning to Julie with the whispered translation. "Franz thinks you're very pretty."

"How kind of him," she whispered back, smiling nervously and nodding her acknowledgement of the compliment to Franz Jantner.

The men began their discourse. Dieter seemed to be doing most of the talking, interrupted now and then by some terse remark from Jan. Julie could not understand a word of what was being said but, on the whole, the tone sounded agreeable enough.

Jantner fascinated her, as did his son. She wondered abstractedly how the older man had come by the tracery of scars that criss-crossed his face, and if he would be too sensitive about them to be photographed before they left this place.

The conversation ended some thirty minutes later and, when Julie went back into the convent, the pale-faced Frau Sedlacek was waiting for her. She seemed excited and ushered Julie down the hall to the antiquated bathroom. The ancient bath had been cleaned and a row of steaming buckets had been laid out in a row. Thanking the woman, Julie bathed herself with relief, not caring about the unsophistication of it all as she poured the refreshing water over her tired body. And, when she was finished, she found the little Karol waiting for her outside the door.

It was a strange party that dined together that night. The sun had long set behind the trees yet it was barely any cooler.

A large, grey pot had been set before them. Inside it was the now-familiar paprika-flavoured stew and, as she ate, Julie also recognised the taste of fish.

"How do you like it?" Jan asked, as she ladled from the pot for a second helping.

Julie nodded vigorously. "It's very good."

When the meal was over, Helga retired into the guest room as Jan and Dieter excused themselves and returned to the house of Franz Jantner. Julie sat on the veranda alone. Alone, that is, except for Karol. She looked down the street at the now silent village and felt again that strong surge of excitement. It was hard to believe she was really here, glimpsing into the unknown realms of a country that held so much to itself; held itself so secretly, and so dangerously.

A movement behind her made her turn. A young woman was standing there, holding a small baby. She called softy to Karol and, as he ran towards her, Julie stood up, smiling into the shy face of the Rumanian girl. The boy pointed a finger upwards at the girl and told her, "Mama."

Julie spoke quietly to the girl in English, "You have a fine son in Karol."

The girl seemed to understand and her smile widened. She nodded her head and took his hand before turning and disappearing into the darkness of the village. It was sometime later when Julie heard the heavy convent door open and close, and then the voice of Jan Sometski coming from the hallway. He was talking quietly, and to someone whose voice Julie did not recognise.

* * *

In Jantner's house, Dieter and the Rumanian sat together at a round, wooden table and spoke softly in German.

"Satisfied, Franz?" The German heaved up his huge bulk. "It is good news, is it not, that the English girl wishes to visit Moldova."

The Rumanian nodded. "I have already contacted my people at Uj."

Dieter smiled slyly. He knew that no-one had a greater desire for money than this Rumanian village elder. It was for that reason alone that he could depend entirely upon his loyalty.

"You realise," Dieter went on, "that the more sophisticated stuff will have to be flown in? There's only so much that I can carry in my two trucks, and that must be well hidden by the charity stuff — especially with a TV crew in tow. Can you arrange it?"

"Leave it to me. The arrangements have already been made."

The two men shook hands and Dieter left. He opened the convent door quietly so as not to awaken the others. And, as he made his way upstairs, he heard a movement behind him and saw Julie coming from the bathroom.

"Ah, Julie," he said. "Are you finding it hard to sleep?"

Her blue eyes turned and held his, cold and uninviting. "I'm fine, Dieter."

"Perhaps a little company might help?"

Julie turned sharply away and Dieter smiled. The Pole had good taste. And it could turn out to be not only a profitable trip this time, but an interesting one as well . . .

In her room, Julie took out some paper and a pen and wrote a long letter to her father. Afterwards, when she could find nothing more to say, she slipped it into an envelope and laid it on a table by the side of the lumpy, iron cot.

Lying there, her thoughts drifted to

Jan. She pictured him sleeping, and his shoulders bathed in silver by the moonlight. She turned on her side and tried to sleep, grateful for the silence of the night.

4

THE next morning, Julie read the letter she had written again. It didn't matter that she may have no way of posting it until she reached a larger town. She was missing her father and, for a while, she needed to feel a little closer to home. Reading it through, she smiled wanly as she realised that, sticking out like a sore thumb, was her undoubted attraction to Jan Sometski.

She slipped it back into the envelope and glanced towards the sleeping Helga. In repose, the German girl's face was even more beautiful. Her hair tumbled onto the pillow as she lay in the half-light, sleek and mysterious, and reminding Julie of a sleeping cat.

She shook her head, getting up and throwing on a robe. There was only one bucket waiting for her in the bathroom this morning and she knew she was lucky to get even that! Water was a scarce commodity in these outlying villages. There were no mains here! And without much rain, the wells soon dried up.

When she was dressed, she strolled downstairs to find the two cars parked outside. Jan was bent over one of them, packing their stuff into the boot while Ben and Jack were loading up the other. Jan glanced up at her approach and she was conscious of the sudden jolt of her heart as his eyes lit on her. It's force surprised her. In the past she had been briefly in love, but had never felt quite like this!

He straightened up. "Did you sleep OK?" he greeted her.

She nodded, murmuring, "Like a log."

"All set for Uj?"

"Yes, I think so. What time are we leaving?"

Jan sighed, glancing briefly at his watch. "I'd intended to be off by nine,

80

but knowing those two," he nodded towards the convent's upper windows, "it will probably be noon before they're ready."

"Who?"

"Dieter and Helga."

"Are they coming with us?"

"Dieter insists on it!"

"Why? What would interest him in Uj-Moldova?"

Jan smiled grimly. "Apparently, he wants to fix up another route for his relief aid in case Rumania gets sucked into another Balkans war."

"I see."

Julie masked her disappointment and glanced across at the second car. She knew the two television engineers would be going to Moldova with them, but she hadn't expected anyone else. Especially Helga and Dieter!

She walked slowly on. The village seemed deserted this morning now that the rest of the aid convoy had left, setting off at first light for an orphanage somewhere farther north. At the convent gates, Franz Jantner was allocating tins of food and blankets to an anxious group of people and, darting amongst the excited children, Julie spotted Karol as he helped his mother.

She glanced up at the two helicopters that were circling overhead.

"We've been warned to look out for trouble," she heard Jan say quietly as he came up behind her.

She turned quickly, her eyes widening. "What kind of trouble?"

"A couple of armed jeeps have been spotted on the mountain road and they might be after the supplies — especially the drugs." He flicked his head upwards towards the sky. "That's why the choppers are here — they're looking out for them."

Julie grimaced. "Then let's hope they find them."

But even as she spoke, another sound came to her ears. The crackle of automatic fire came from the south side of the village and everyone was suddenly fleeing for shelter. Jan's strong arm shot out, dragging Julie into the safety of the convent's wall as the thud of mortar fire became suddenly ominous.

"Keep down," he rasped.

Frozen with fear, Julie ducked low and Jan's arms came around her like a shield. They clung together for what seemed an age while the sounds of the gunfire advanced and receded around them. Vaguely, she could hear voices screaming, and the sound of running feet as the villagers scattered for safer cover, then she heard the screech of tyres less than a few feet away.

After fifteen minutes or so of frantic mayhem she heard Jan's voice come hoarsely in her ear, "I think it's OK now. It sounds like they're going."

Julie listened. The sounds of fighting were fading now, leaving only a strong smell of carbide pervading the air. She shifted her position lifting her head slightly and brushing away the small cloud of white dust as it flurried from her hair, loosened by the mortars that had shaken the sheltering, pock-marked wall.

Jan straightened up, peering round with trained caution and then beckoning to her to hurry after him.

"Come on! Let's move!"

They ran, half-crouching, back up the street towards the gates. The crowd had gathered again and were huddled over something on the ground and, Julie noticed, Karol's young mother was on her knees beside it, weeping unrestrainedly.

Then her heart stopped as she recognised the small bundle at the girl's feet, suddenly conscious that Karol had been hurt. And, in a blur, she saw the terrible wound the boy had suffered to his leg.

"Oh, no!"

The tense expression came from Jan as he swept past the others and knelt beside the boy. "Make way! Let me see!" His voice lashed at Julie like a whip. "Get one of the medics! Tell him to radio the base at Tulcea! Tell him what's happened and tell him we need a helicopter!"

Julie fled up the convent's winding path, running for the boy's life. Behind her came confused cries but she was too shocked to care. Now, Julie had one driving passion! Nothing must happen to Karol!

A young medic, alerted by the cries, was already in the doorway and she called out urgently, "Phone the base at Tulcea — a child's been hit — "

"We already have!" he answered, sprinting towards Jan and the boy.

Julie turned, looking for Karol's white-faced mother. But then, as they carried the boy inside, she saw that Franz Jantner was already with her, helping her into the hallway and offering an arm of comfort.

"Did you manage to get through to Tulcea?" Jan asked the medic grimly as he kneeled beside the boy.

"Yes."

"Anyone else hurt?"

"No — a few people are suffering from shock but they'll be OK."

"Any idea who the gunmen were?"

"It's anybody's guess. But they got what they came for."

"The drugs?"

The medic nodded, soaking a white pad with antiseptic lotion and wiping it along Karol's leg. "Three crates of 'em."

Jan frowned. He'd known, somehow, that the medical supplies had been the attraction. Then, his frown deepening, he turned his attention back to the boy's wounds. "He needs a hospital. We haven't the equipment here and he's lost a lot of blood."

"Is there a hospital at Tulcea?" Julie asked, kneeling beside Jan and taking a handful of cotton wool from the medic's pouch to wipe Karol's forehead.

"There's a clinic of sorts but it couldn't handle this," Jan answered grimly. "He'd be lucky if they could find him an aspirin. We'll alert Bucharest and fly him down there. With a bit of luck — he should make it in time — "

Julie watched Jan's pale face as he helped clean the boy's wounds, and his gaunt expression was telling her that he'd seen it all before.

"Lucky we were here," he muttered bitterly. "He'd never have made it otherwise."

Julie nodded and glanced across at the boy's mother who was still weeping silently as she leaned against Franz. "How long do you think it will take for them to get here?"

"If there's one already available, fifteen minutes should do it. If not — and Mac has to radio for one — " He shrugged. "Who knows?"

"Who's Mac . . . ?"

"The guy who runs the base — an American."

Julie glanced again at the boy. His blank, semi-conscious eyes stared back at her, becoming more confused and terrified as the minutes dragged by.

Then her heart leaped at the sound

of a helicopter and, glancing through the open doorway, Julie watched as the it touched down in the centre of the village.

The American was short, barrel-chested, and an unlit cigar was clenched tightly between his teeth. His face was brown, like a walnut, and his greying hair curled tightly around his ears.

"I've let them know in Bucharest, it's all set up," Mac O'Reilly said as he came into the convent and shook Jan's outstretched hand. "Lilly's with me. She'll stay with the boy and his mother all the way."

Jan nodded brusquely. And when, between them, they had carried Karol out to the helicopter and settled him inside with his mother, Julie saw a woman's face appear momentarily at the porthole's window as she signalled to the men.

Mac O'Reilly grinned. "Lilly sends her love."

"Give her mine back."

"Right! We'll be off. And, don't worry, everything's on hand."

"Don't waste any time, Mac, the boy's in a bad way."

"I can see that." O'Reilly glanced at Sometski sharply. "Leave him to us now — he'll be OK." He climbed back on board. "Take care, you hear?"

Jan nodded and stood back as the rotors began to spin. "I will."

Suddenly, Julie ran forward. "Please! One second!" She thrust her hand deep into her pocket, bringing out the creased envelope that contained the letter to her father. "I know it's a bad time but, if you do get the chance, would you post this for me in Bucharest? It's — it's for my father."

Mac O'Reilly reached out for the letter, glancing cursorily at the address. "Sure, no problem." He turned briefly back to Jan, stuffing Julie's letter into his trouser pocket. "See you, Jan. Don't worry about the boy, he's in good hands with us."

The helicopter's rotors accelerated

and O'Reilly gave a final wave as they gained altitude. Jan and Julie watched as it circled above them before disappearing over the mountains on its way to Tulcea. When it was out of sight Jan turned, his face white with strain and he reached into his breast pocket and took a long swig of brandy from a small, silver flask.

"Poor little devil," he muttered grimly, wiping a hand across his mouth and pocketing the flask. "All we can do now is pray."

"I didn't know about the air base," she said quietly as they made their way back up the street to the convent. "I wonder if Dad knows about it."

Jan looked at her, hands thrust into his pockets and a frown on his face. "More than likely," he answered, "all the news agencies use it. It's quicker than Bucharest — less red tape. And we know how much the Press hate to waste time when they're covering all the insanities that are going on around here."

"You sound bitter."

"I am!"

She smiled slightly. "Well, at least you don't mince your words."

"Anything for a story, eh? And the bloodier it is, the better!"

"Sometimes, perhaps . . . " Julie agreed softly. "And for what good it does, I've told my boss what I think about it — that we should perhaps be a little more human in the way we cover ours."

"Your boss being your father?" His voice was sharp.

She shot him a look. "I've spoken to more people than my father and Harry Green about sensitive coverage!"

Julie flopped down on an old, dead stump and ran her hands through her hair, sighing deeply. Jan sat down beside her.

"Well, that makes two of us!" Jan went on. "Trouble is, people are getting conditioned to all the war news that's about today."

"I know." Her response came flat

and weary. "That's why I want to do my story right."

He didn't answer for a while, the silence stretching between them, until he said quietly, "It really matters to you, doesn't it?"

"Yes, it does."

He turned to her curiously, "So how can a place like Uj-Moldova grab your viewers interest? How can your film about it help?"

She stood up, straightening her skirt. "It can't! But it may help if I can show them that we are all part of the same world and we must all do our best." She got to her feet and started to move away. "And at least I feel I'm doing something," she went on, "and not just sitting at home in England merely talking about it!"

He slipped an arm lightly around her shoulder, saying quietly, "Good for you, Julie Stiller."

They walked on for a while in silence, then Julie looked up. "This pilot friend of yours, Mac O'Reilly . . . How did you come to know him?"

"I met him when I was covering the trouble in Armenia," he answered casually. "Mac was there, too, working for the Washington Post. Consequently, we bumped into each other a couple of times."

"And Lilly?"

"His wife. She used to be a nurse." Jan grinned slightly. "Mac was always in the thick of things. The time he met Lilly he'd hired a clapped-out old plane to cover a story on the field hospitals — a sort of Armenian version of M.A.S.H." He smiled crookedly and then went on, "She happened to be working in one of them at the time and so they met. They got married in America, and then, when the barriers came down and the free-market opened up, they both moved back to here — to Lilly's place — and opened up a business together."

Julie looked up, surprised. "An American open up a business in Eastern Europe? Could he do that?"

His grin widened. "Mac did! When the Russians went away a lot of their stuff was left behind and, somehow Mac managed to acquire some of it — including a couple of helicopters. He and Lilly set about building up a private transport company at the old army base at Tulcea."

"You mean, he took over an army base just like that?"

He nodded again. "Just like that! No-one was using it."

"I see . . . "

"Mac's always been an opportunist," Jan went on. "He's smart and he could see that there were huge profits to be made here in providing faster — more efficient transport and Tulcea's in an absolutely ideal spot."

"Where is Tulcea?"

"On the Black Sea coast. They've done quite well, so far. And he's helped me out a couple of times, too." He glanced across at the group of villagers who had started to clear up the damage in the street. "Anyway, shall we make ourselves useful and give them a hand?"

"Yes, I think we should."

"We might as well. We won't be going to Uj today. This little lot's completely blown our schedule."

5

JULIE eased herself up, feeling the ache in her back from the uncomfortable bed as she swung herself out of it and glanced across at Helga. She was puzzled. The girl had been missing for most of the night. And when she had finally heard her creep back into their room, the pale light of dawn was already touching the sky.

Helga stirred, opening her eyes and staring blankly up at the high, white-painted ceiling. She looked terrible this morning and, suddenly, Julie had an uncomfortable feeling of foreboding.

"Are you all right?" she asked, pausing by the bed.

The girl sat up. "Yes," she replied, her voice little more than a croak in her throat. "I'm still tired, that's all. Leave me alone."

Julie sighed, used now to Helga's

ungraciousness. And, moments later, as she wandered into the washroom, she wondered again what could have kept her out so late. And later still, when she went back into the room, she found that Helga had not moved.

"Better stir yourself, Helga," she said. "Jan wants an early start to make up for the time we lost yesterday."

"I'm not coming."

Julie swung round. "What did you say?"

"I said I'm not coming. I'm, I'm ill — I have a temperature."

Julie stared at her for a moment. True enough, Helga did look pale. "What's the matter?" she asked. "How do you feel?"

The girl glared. "I've already told you! I feel ill! Too ill to travel to Moldova!"

"Then you'd better let Dieter know — "

"I already know — " There was a sound behind her and Julie turned abruptly to see Dieter standing in the half-opened doorway. He came in and

97

stood by Helga's bed, looking down at her with a rather mocking smile. "It's nothing serious, is it, my love? Nothing that a little rest wouldn't cure?"

Julie looked again at the unsmiling Helga Bauer. "But we can't leave her here alone, surely?"

"Why not? It's what she wants."

"But, will she be all right? I mean — suppose there's more trouble?"

"There won't be."

Julie stared at Dieter in amazement. "You sound very sure of it."

"I am."

"But — how can you be so sure? Hadn't we better phone Mac again? If Helga's ill, surely she would be better off at Tulcea."

"Oh, do be quiet!" Helga reached for a cigarette, muttering tensely, "I'll be fine. It's better that I stay here."

Julie wanted to continue her argument. After all, she didn't want the responsibility of a sick woman on their hands on top of everything else. But privately, she knew, too, that she could do nothing.

And she couldn't force the girl if she really preferred to stay.

Her stomach gave a lurch. Instinct was telling her that Helga's sudden illness was deceptive. Had her absence last night had anything to do with it? The German girl was pale — that was true enough — but, she didn't seem as ill as she was making herself out to be.

Julie shrugged inwardly, wondering why Helga was going to such lengths to stay behind. "Well, if you're sure," she murmured, stuffing her night things into the canvas bag and zipping it up.

She went outside. Jan was already waiting in the car and, beyond the gates she could see that Ben and Jack had set about packing their recording gear again. And, as she approached, Jan swung out and took her bag, finding room for it in the boot.

"Is that it?" he asked.

Julie nodded. "Yes, that's the lot. But Helga's ill, did you know?"

He inclined his head, his face

expressionless. "So Dieter informs me."

"I don't like the idea of leaving her here on her own."

"Neither do I. But Dieter will have Jantner take care of her. He's no doubt given him his orders."

"Dieter seems to have a lot of influence in this place."

"He does! He oils the wheels and he pays them well. They like his money and they'll do as he asks." Jan frowned and turned away.

"But what sort of things does he pay them for?"

"I don't know yet, but I intend to find out." He threw her a small grin. "Anyway, that's my problem, so don't you start to worry about it. And don't worry about Helga, either. She'll be OK."

"I hope so."

Ignoring her bleak expression, Jan went on quietly, "I don't like it any more than you do. But don't forget, Helga is Dieter's responsibility — you are mine!"

Jan strode around the car and checked out the engine. He hadn't enjoyed giving Julie the impression that he condoned Dieter's ways, but there was nothing he could do about it now! What was the matter with him? It was as though he wanted the girl's approval!

Julie shrugged, frowning back at the convent with slight misgivings. She saw Dieter come out and walk hurriedly towards Franz Jantner's house and, as he reached it, the Rumanian opened the door and handed the German a heavy, leather bag. Then, for several minutes, the two men went into a deep conversation before the Rumanian nodded briefly and went back inside.

Dieter turned and made his way over to the car, placing the leather bag beside him as he heaved himself into the back seat.

Across the square, Jack and Ben gave Jan the thumbs-up that they were all ready to move, and he waved them on. And then, as they followed after them, Julie gave a final glance to the convent and saw the shadowed form of Helga watching them from the upstairs window.

From his seat in the back, Dieter must have followed her gaze. "Don't worry about my Helga," Julie heard him murmur softly. "I know she has her reasons for staying behind."

"Do you, Dieter?" Julie countered coldly. "I hope so . . . "

When they moved off, the day was already hot and still and the air held that head-aching oppressiveness that always precedes a storm. Not one of them, it seemed, was in the mood for conversation — as if the effort was too much — and so, silently, they journeyed north, progressing at a steady rate along a reasonably good main road.

After almost two hours, Jan swung off on to a narrower road and, from then on, the going became more tough. The heat of the day had become unbearable now, and to make matters worse, their progress was impeded by the countless carts and herds of animals that never seemed to end.

Julie shifted her position, glancing out of the window at the row upon row of birch trees, then she looked upwards into the distance, and at the bleak, dark outline of the Carpathian mountains. Seeing them so close made her smile a little, remembering how her grandfather used to tell her of the times when, as a boy when it was winter, he would ski along those steep, silent slopes.

"How far are we from Uj?" Dieter's voice came from the back.

"About four hours — maybe less."

"Can you stop? I need a break."

"OK." Jan smiled and slowed the car. "Will this do?"

"This is fine."

Flashing his lights at the other car as a signal for them to go on without them, Jan pulled in towards a glade. And, as soon as the engine stilled Dieter opened the door, his hand still clutching the bag and muttering that he'd be back in a moment. And, as the man disappeared in to the forest, Jan looked across at Julie.

"Feel like stretching your legs, too?" he asked.

"No, I'm fine," she answered. "It's nice to sit here and feel the breeze."

"Yes, I suppose it is."

Jan observed her silently. There was a grace in the way she sat, her camera on her lap and her hand coiled loosely around her denimed knee. He liked the eager sparkle of her eyes as she looked once more up to the mountains. He noticed the fine tanning of her skin from the Rumanian summer sun, and the way her blonde hair was curling round her face.

He turned away, glad that she did not notice — or feel — his aching, hungry eyes upon her. And, when she next looked at him, his eyes were downcast as he frowned in thought.

"I suppose I should warn you," he said quietly, "you'll only have me for company in Uj tonight."

"Oh?"

He grinned. "Ben and Jack are driving on to Bacao — Ben knows somebody there. And Dieter, apparently, has his charity business to attend to."

Julie heard the grimness in his tone and threw him a curious glance. "Don't you believe him?"

He shrugged, still frowning. "No, I don't. I think he's up to something."

"Such as?"

"I wish I knew. But something doesn't smell right about all this. I know Bermann of old! It's not in his nature to be so involved out of the goodness of his heart. He loves the colour of money too much!"

"But how can he make money here? I mean, the people are so poor and — " She broke off suddenly as a dark thought struck her, then she said slowly, "The relief aid — He couldn't be involved in some sort of black market, could he?"

Jan shrugged again, his eyes serious.

"I don't know — "

"But, surely the authorities — "

"They can't be everywhere, and the black market is rife."

"It's immoral!"

Jan held her angry gaze. "I know. And, what's worse is I can't prove anything — I've already tried."

They both fell silent as Dieter came back, then as the darkening sky suddenly cracked with lightning, Jan looked up.

"Here it comes," he mumbled, "I was hoping to be in Uj before the storm broke."

Suddenly, the rain came down in a torrent, drenching everything around them in seconds. It was so heavy Julie could hardly see a thing in front of her and, as they set off once again, the wipers could barely clear the deluge from the windscreen. The wind whipped at the treetops and the lightning flashed again, whitening their shapes like a brilliant torch.

The storm passed as quickly as it

had come but, held up for ages by a convoy of farm machinery, it was early evening before they finally drove along the main street of Uj-Moldova.

For Julie, seeing the place for the very first time, it was almost like coming back home. The dark, forested mountains with their craggy peaks were evocative of legend, and they overshadowed the town of her grandparents birth. Some places have a magic all their own and, for Julie, this was such a place.

Her eyes darted everywhere. Even in the fading light she could see that it was beautiful! The land and rock glowed crimson in the setting sun, and a river flowed silently past the remains of an old Turkish castle, its reflection shimmering in the water.

There were a few people about, some on the horse-drawn ploughs she had seen so often in her grandparents yellowed pictures. As they drove further down the sloping street Julie saw an old, stone bridge, and she wondered if it was the same bridge her grandmother had told her of and of how the shepherd counted each of his sheep as they crossed it one by one, and of how he never stayed awake long enough to count them all.

When they reached the square, Jan pulled up outside an inn, and eagerly, Julie stepped out of the car. She stood reflectively for a moment, looking down the tree-lined street and remembering . . .

Ilona Listl and Lajos Stiller had been born here. They had grown up here, fallen in love here, and would have married here if the war had not scattered them, dispersing their families like so many fallen leaves. As it was they married in England and never came back. If the war hadn't happened, they would probably both have been buried here, too.

She gave a deep, deep sigh. So this was the Banat! Her grandparents home! Fleetingly, the faded photograph of her grandmother crept back into her mind. She saw again the pretty, young girl with the crown of bright, plaited hair, and the blue, slightly-slanting eyes that had been her inheritance to her granddaughter.

But then, breaking into her thoughts, she heard Jan call her name and she came back to earth with a bump.

Inside the inn, and past a pleasant, outdoor terrace, Julie found herself in a surprisingly comfortable, rustic lounge. And, leaving her briefly in the middle of the hall, Jan went to speak to a man behind the desk.

Dieter, she noticed, was still standing by the doorway, and still holding tightly to the leather bag. But now, to her surprise and forming a semi-circle around him, were four young men who seemed to have appeared from nowhere to greet him.

"Looks like Dieter's business has already begun," she murmured wryly as she went to stand by Jan at the desk. "What do you think all that is about?"

Jan threw a brief glance in their direction. "I've no idea," he conceded grimly. "But they knew he was coming, that's for sure."

"What do you think he's got in that bag? Money?"

"I can't think what else it can be."

Dieter glanced across at them, almost as though he'd overheard. Strangely, a tension was starting to grow inside Julie. And suspecting that Dieter might be up to something shady was already making her feel nervous.

She made a silent vow. When she got back home, she would make sure there would be an investigation into his so-called charity work.

Dieter strolled over. "You will excuse me this evening?"

"Of course!"

The German turned away and followed the four young men outside, leaving her alone with Jan. She turned to him, frowning, "What do you think they're up to?"

"Your guess is as good as mine.

But, it is my intention to find out before too long." The man behind the desk handed him some keys and he turned back to Julie with a grin, his deep voice dry. "In the meantime, shall we freshen up and have a little dinner?"

"Good idea."

"Afterwards, we'll find something to do."

Julie laughed, looking around at the tiny, quiet inn. "I've a feeling there won't be much choice."

He shrugged and grinned again. "I agree. But we could go for a walk if you like, see if your grandfather's house is still there."

Julie shook her head. "It isn't. It was destroyed a long time ago — during the war. But I'd like to look at the church if that's OK. My great-grandparents are buried there."

Jan frowned slightly. "I think you may be disappointed. Most of the old graves have gone, I'm afraid, after all the shelling that went on around here.

It's likely your family's grave was one of them."

Julie's face fell, "I see." But then she looked up at him and added with a smile, "Well, never mind, I'll put some flowers inside the church — it will be almost the same, won't it?"

He nodded, saying, "And, if you like, when you've done that, we'll walk by the river."

They went upstairs to their rooms. And, as Julie opened her door she could see at once that this was a vast improvement on her previous room at the convent. It was lighter and airier and, as she placed her hands upon it and felt its spring, guessed that the bed was softer, too. But, pinned behind the door, a time-check list told her that the water here was still a problem.

She washed and changed quickly and then went back downstairs to find Jan waiting for her at the bar.

"Hungry?" he asked, taking her arm and leading her into the red-shaded dining-room.

"Starving."

But, hungry as she was, dinner turned out to be a disappointment. It was poorly cooked and tasteless, and even the ubiquitous goulash seemed to have been prised out of a tin. Afterwards, when they had washed it down with a very good wine, they went outside to take their walk.

The moon was bright and the night was still as they started up towards the little church. Clutching a spray of wild flowers, gathered from the fields, they went inside and gently, Julie placed them on the altar. She kneeled down in front of it for a moment or two in remembrance of her family, and then, after closing the door softly behind them, she and Jan continued their walk to the river.

She was very conscious of the man by her side and she wondered about him. He was telling her of Poland, and of his family there. And of how, he'd been to visit them now that his country, like Rumania, had opened its borders to the world. He was telling her, too, of his love for Scotland, and of how it seemed to be the only place where he truly found some peace.

He seemed so alone. And, listening to his deep, attractive voice washing over her, Julie wanted more than anything for him to take her into his arms. She knew he would be wonderful! But, she knew too, that if he should — for the first time in her life — she wouldn't know how to handle it.

"Are you tired?" he was asking, breaking through her thoughts.

Julie shook her head. "No, not a bit. Why, do I seem to be?"

Jan laughed softly, "Well, it was either that or I was boring you to death. You're very quiet — hardly said a word."

"I'm sorry. I was interested in what you were saying, that's all."

He laughed again and placed an arm around her shoulders. "Flattery will get your everywhere, Julie Stiller. Fancy a nightcap?"

Julie smiled her agreement and, comfortably, they made their way back to the inn. But then, as they sat together in a corner with their glass of beer, Julie's heart suddenly sank as the bulky form of Dieter appeared through the doorway, three of the Moldovans following behind.

The German seemed in high spirits as he came and sat beside them. "Had a nice time, you two?"

Jan looked at him, his face grim. "You look pleased with yourself, Dieter. I take it your business was a success."

Julie glanced from one man to the other, comparing the heavy German with the lean and beautiful Jan and thought how very different — in every way — the two men were.

"Complete success," Dieter was saying, his features creased into what passed as a smile. "But I'm tired now. Dealing with these people can be hard work. I'm off to my room — it's been a long day."

He finished off his beer and stood

up, dismissing the Moldovans with a brief wave of his hand before leaving the bar and going up to his room, the leather bag still tucked safely under his arm.

The Moldovans left, too, all except one, that is. He remained where he was, standing impassively by the bar and, for some strange reason, as she caught the man's eye, Julie shivered.

There was a threat in his silent presence and it frightened her. It was as though this strange, silent stranger was the harbinger of trouble to come.

6

UPSTAIRS in his room, Dieter lay down on the bed and cupped his hands around his head. He smiled complacently. His business had been profitable tonight and there should be more to come. Perhaps his luck would continue.

A short time ago he had heard Jan Sometski and Julie Stiller bidding each other a tender good-night outside his door and he smiled darkly to himself. What a handsome pair they made! And they could despise him all they liked but, without him, they would not get very far!

He sat up and lit a cigarette, his mind drifting to Julie Stiller. He could understand the Pole's interest in the girl — he was attracted to her, too. She was different than most women he had known. She held that aloofness he so admired and, sitting there, Dieter began to draw pleasure in his study of her. He lay silently thoughtful for a few more minutes, and then he got up and went out, crossing the passage to her room.

Julie looked up as she answered the soft tap on her door, disappointment shadowing her eyes as Dieter Bermann came in. She had thought it was Jan but now, seeing that it wasn't, she cursed inwardly and prayed he would soon go away.

"What do you want, Dieter?" she asked, swinging her legs from off the bed.

"I want to talk to you — "

"What about? It's very late." Her tone was weary, and she had nothing to say to the German.

"It's about Sometski. It's important."

"Can't it wait until morning?"

"It can. But it's better that we talk now while everyone's asleep."

Julie sighed deeply, standing up and throwing on her dressing-gown.

Whatever this man had to say, Julie knew she wouldn't like it.

"Well, make it quick, Dieter — I'm tired."

Dieter Bermann stepped further into the room, his cold eyes regarding Julie in an alarming way.

"You'll thank me for it," he murmured.

She replied calmly, "I doubt it, but get it off your chest anyway."

"I am fond of Jan, he is my friend," he began, moving closer to her. "I respect him in many ways, but there are things that you should know about him and — "

Julie edged away. "Is this how you show your respect — your friendship? Talking about him behind his back?"

He grinned, his eyes narrowing and then the German went on, "I like you, Julie. I do not want to see you hurt."

"That's very considerate of you, Dieter. But before you say anything more, I think I should warn you that Sometski is my friend, too! And I am particularly loyal to those I care for!"

119

He nodded. "Very noble."

"Besides, why should he want to hurt me?"

"Because he will, it is his way — "

Impatiently she turned away. "Really, Dieter! I have no wish to listen to this kind of talk."

He raised a placating hand. "No, hear me. I know Sometski. He is playing with you, and it is convenient that you are on hand for him."

"Look! I've already told you I don't want to hear any of this!"

"But you should. I know him better than you. Surely, you do not want to waste your time with someone who does not care, when I could give you so much?"

Julie's throat was suddenly bone dry. She stepped back, putting distance between herself and the offensive German. He wasn't smiling now. He was showing no emotion at all, and his voice was silky no longer.

She moved towards the door and put her hand on the catch, suddenly wary.

There was something about him that was putting her on her guard. "It's late! Go to bed, Dieter."

Dieter made no move. "I am thinking only of you," he said softly. "Sometski is handsome, yes? What girl could resist him? And you are . . . available . . . ?"

He moved towards her, reaching out his hand to stroke her hair.

Julie felt nauseated. How could she allow Dieter to go on like this? She closed her eyes, shutting out the man's words as he went on, "I am warning you of him for another reason . . . " The unfeeling eyes glittered as he looked down at her. "Allow me to tell you a little story. There was a girl once, and her name was Anna — "

That was enough for Julie! Her eyes became bright with hot, uncontrollable temper. "Will you get out of here, Dieter? You've said quite enough!"

Dieter smiled. He had touched a nerve. And at last he had cracked the composure. "I want you to know that you have Dieter to protect you."

She laughed scornfully. "You!"

"Yes, liebchen." He stroked her arm, moving closer. "Be sensible, Julie. I am powerful and wealthy. I could give you everything."

Tiny beads of perspiration were beginning to break out all over her body and she stepped back against the door. His hand touched her right arm and she felt it shaking as his grip on her tightened, pulling her into his arms.

"Go back to your room, Dieter," she urged, squirming away from him. "Leave me alone!"

He smiled winningly. "Now, let's be sensible. Isn't this a perfect time to get to know each other better?"

Suddenly Julie was scared — very scared. Her arms, held by Dieter's grip, were hurting and, as she tried to cry out, the words choked in her throat. She tried again to pull away but he held her fast. Fear pumped her adrenalin and she summoned all her strength to free her arms, but her movements were restricted and she had no power to move.

A mist was dancing in front of her eyes now, red and hot. She tried again to scream, but no sound came. Then, just as reality seemed to fade, she heard Jan's voice outside the door,

"Julie!"

Every prayer she had uttered in all her life must have been answered in that one split second. Dieter fell back, loosening his hold and she swung round to pull open the door. "Jan! Come in! Come in!"

But Jan's eyes narrowed as he saw Dieter standing here. "What's going on here?" he asked coldly, looking first at one and then the other. "What are you doing here, Dieter?"

"Dieter was just about to leave, weren't you, Dieter?" Julie opened the door wider, her eyes glaring at the German, repeating in a louder tone, "Weren't you, Dieter?"

"If you insist, my little one." Dieter's

smile was mocking as he moved towards the door, saying with heavy sarcasm, "Your timing, Jan, as always, is quite impeccable."

Jan took a step forward and grabbed his shoulder.

"I asked, what was going on?"

Dieter shrugged. "It is nothing," he said, turning awkwardly away. "Julie got a little hysterical, that's all. I only wished to talk."

Jan's grip tightened on the man's shoulder. "I should have known not to turn my back."

Bermann shrugged himself out of Jan's hold. "This is ridiculous."

"Is it, Dieter?" Jan glared at the German, "I don't think so. I think it's time you and I had a quiet talk. I have a few questions that need a few answers." He turned briefly to Julie, telling her calmly. "Go to my room, Julie, and wait for me there!"

But then Julie gasped, taking a step forward as she saw Dieter's bunched fist aim for Jan's solar plexis and she cried out a warning. "Jan! Jan! Look out!"

Sometski turned back quickly to see Dieter's fist lunging towards him and he swerved away out of reach. Then, suddenly, the whole scene erupted as Jan hit out against Bermann's chest, winding him, and causing the German to fall back, stumbling against a chair.

Sometski's face was stony and hard as he pulled the man to his feet. "This is the last time, Bermann . . . "

And, with his hands still gripped around Dieter's throat, he turned once more to Julie,

"Go to my room, Julie!"

"But, Jan, I want to — "

"Look, Julie, for once would you simply do as I ask."

Julie did as Jan asked and, as she sat on a chair by the bed, she went over what had happened. She couldn't contain the revulsion that ran through her.

Eventually, Jan came to join her in the room.

"Here, drink this." His voice was strained but concerned.

Sometski handed the flask to Julie, but she shook her head, not wanting anything.

She glanced vaguely up at Jan. "What happened to Dieter? Where is he?"

"He's back in his room, there shouldn't be any more trouble from him tonight."

Julie looked up towards Sometski. His face was still and thoughtful and, as he turned away unsmiling, he caught her glance.

"How do you feel now?" he asked.

She smiled a little wanly. "I'm OK, I suppose."

"You have been lucky tonight. Whatever possessed you to let that man into your room?"

Julie made no response, her face very still. She was deep in thought. Did Jan think she had encouraged Dieter? Did he think he'd been there at her request? It just wasn't fair! Sometski was distant now, hardly speaking. Perhaps he did

126

believe it had all been her fault. And, so far at least, he hadn't explained why he had knocked on her door at so late an hour, either.

Julie answered bleakly. "Yes, I suppose I was lucky tonight."

"As soon as Ben and Jack come back from Bacau in the morning, we'll get this filming over and done with and then get you safely home," he told her quietly. "For now, lock your door and try to get some sleep." Jan moved towards the door, saying as he opened it, "and don't answer it to anyone, not even to me." He fought back the urge to add . . . "especially to me!"

★ ★ ★

By Franz Jantner's door, the young Rumanian lifted his head as he watched Helga Bauer walk towards him from the convent. He stood silent and immobile, waiting for her like a dark shadow. He was seventeen, and already a man. The fighting in Bosnia had seen to that.

The girl moved slowly towards him and, when she reached him, she asked in German, "Nicolas, did you do as I asked?"

The boy's eyes narrowed. He had quarrelled with his father about this woman and it was irresponsible of him to keep on seeing her like this and to ignore Franz Jantner's warning, but he could not help himself.

His hand reached out to touch her mouth and he answered her slowly in her language, "I did as you asked."

"Excellent." Helga laughed softly, her time had come. Then the laughter faded and she became serious again. "Are they here?"

The youth nodded again and opened the door, ushering Helga forward. Once inside, they talked for a little over half an hour. Then, when they had finished, the boy handed her some papers and she smiled up into the young, dark eyes. "You have done well, Nicolas. You have followed Dieter and your father, and now you have given me the proof I need. I shall see that you are rewarded. Is the car ready for me?"

The boy nodded abruptly. "I have left it where you said."

"Good. Then I have the time to give you your reward."

An hour later, Helga was on her way to Uj. It had been worth spending some time with the boy if that was the price of his bribery. Helga smiled coldly. And it was as well that he had inherited his father's love of money.

Everything had been prepared. And, as the car sped northwards along the deserted road, Helga took a hand off the wheel and fingered the precious papers that were nestling against her skin.

Triumph lit her eyes. This would surely bring Sometski back to her and she laughed out loud as she thought of Dieter. Two for the price of one! Sometski's love and Bermann's ruin. Now all she had to do was be patient for just a little while longer.

★ ★ ★

It was a little after five o'clock in the morning when Helga Bauer finally managed to get word to Jan that she wanted to meet him by the old Turkish castle. A Moldovan boy — the son of her hosts and Nicolas's cousin — had been the messenger. And now, as she watched Jan Sometski's tall shape walking towards her through the dawn's mist, her heart began to beat a little faster.

She had known he would keep this appointment. And after she had told him what she had discovered, he would appreciate all she had done. And, even more importantly, he would see how much more beautiful she was than any of his women.

Helga started at the cry of a waking bird, looking round warily in case it was Dieter who had discovered her arrival. But, when it wasn't, it was in some relief that she turned again to Jan.

130

Her relief might have been more short-lived if she had seen the man. Helga was not aware of the dark shape as it slid into the trees out of her sight. Nor was she aware of the man's face as he hid himself, waiting and listening as she spoke to Jan.

"What is it you want, Helga?" Jan asked briskly as he reached her. "What are you doing here, I thought you were ill? And why all this cloak-and-dagger stuff? Do you know what time it is?"

She beckoned him farther into the shadows. "I have news that will change things for us," she told him softly.

"What do you mean? What news?"

Helga moved closer to Jan, looking up into his face and putting her arms upon his shoulders. "We can have everything, you and I, Jan. I will soon have the means to keep us both in comfort for the rest of our lives."

He pulled her arms away. "What are you talking about?"

"I have discovered things — about Dieter. I have the proof that he is not only selling the aid relief to the black market, but he's supplying arms as well." She smiled up at Jan, putting her hand inside her blouse and pulling out the sheaf of papers, then, her lips curling, she went on slowly, "And there's something else I have found out about Dieter — "

"What?"

"He's dealing in drugs and gold as well. It's all here — his contacts, his payroll, his suppliers! And once I confront him with all my evidence, he will pay me well for my silence, won't he?"

Jan Sometski stared through narrowed eyes at the papers Helga was now holding in her hand. He'd known about the relief aid, and he'd had his suspicions about the drugs and the gun-running. But he had not known about the gold!

"Are those papers genuine?" he asked harshly. "If they are, he's finished. What's in them? Where did you get them from?"

Helga laughed softly. "They're genuine, there's no doubt of that. Dieter doesn't stand a chance now — nor Jantner, because he's in it up to his neck, too. I got all the evidence I needed from Nicolas last night . . . " Helga paused smiling up at him cautiously and pushing the papers back beneath her blouse, her movement causing the dawning light to catch the gold of the locket at her throat. "I did this for us, darling. But, before I show them to you, you must meet my condition."

Jan's frown deepened. "What condition?"

"That you give up the English girl and come back to me."

Jan Sometski stared at her, his expression hardening. "And if I don't?"

She held his gaze, her own expression cold and ruthless. "It would be so easy for me to add your name to that of Dieter's . . . "

Jan smiled faintly. He was in no doubt that Helga meant what she said. She would think nothing of throwing him — and Julie — to the wolves if she did not get her way. He must be cautious.

He answered calmly. "And when do you intend to hand over the list to the authorities?"

Helga smiled again. "Not just yet. Nicolas told me that a plane is due at Tulcea and on board will be two men — Dieter's contacts in the UK. They are bringing in more money, so we might as well have that too, yes?" Helga waited expectantly for Jan's reply, adding softly, "Well, Jan, what do you say?"

Pity for the girl touched Jan briefly. She was playing a dangerous game. For now he would go along with her plan until he held the proof that would bring Bermann and Jantner to justice.

"I'll do as you ask," he said quietly, "but, for safety's sake, you had better let me have the papers."

The girl laughed softly. "Do you really think I am so stupid? No, you can have the papers only when I think the time is right."

"You realise the danger you're in if Dieter finds out?"

"I will hide them safely enough. Now, will you give up the English girl?"

Jan nodded, playing for time. "I have no choice."

Helga nodded smugly. "You will not regret your decision."

"Where are you staying? It is better that you keep out of sight."

"I am staying with Jantner's brother — he knows nothing of this. Don't worry, I will be all right. And I will get word to you when it is safe to meet you again. Now I must go."

He watched her walk away, conscious of the triumph in her eyes as she had lifted her mouth to kiss him.

Helga made her furtive way towards the river, making for the bridge that would take her back into the village.

In the still small hours of the morning no-one noticed the Rumanian enter the inn and arouse the sleeping Dieter. Nor did they see a dark, stealthy form enter another house a little while later. And, as Jan made his own way back to the inn, there was not a sound.

7

JULIE found rest impossible that night. She tossed and turned, counting endless sheep, but all to no avail. Finally, she got up and spent the remaining hours drafting out the script for tomorrow's film. And now, skimming it briefly, she put down her ballpoint and glanced at her watch, heaving a sigh of relief to find that it was already seven o'clock and time for breakfast.

Downstairs, she found Jan alone in the dining-room, sitting morosely at a corner table. And, by the bleary smile he gave her as she went over to join him, Julie suspected that he hadn't slept much last night either.

There was no sign of Dieter, and Julie wasn't sorry. And later, after they had eaten, she and Jan went outside to meet up with the two TV men to make a start on the film.

"I thought we'd shoot the square first," Julie suggested when they were ready to begin, "and then work our way down to the river and finish by that old ruin of a castle. What do you think?"

"Sounds fine to me," Jan answered.

"Make a good final scene," Ben agreed. "You know, Dracula and all that stuff."

Julie laughed. "But he was nowhere near here."

"Doesn't matter, he always turns up somewhere in Rumania, doesn't he?"

They started to film, setting up the camera angles and the sound equipment to record Julie's narration. And as the film progressed Julie couldn't help but notice how edgy Jan appeared to be. She sensed he was disturbed, and wondered if he was still brooding about Dieter's actions in her room last night. And by the time they reached the river, he'd hardly said a word.

"Walk over the bridge, Julie," Jack

called. "Walk towards the castle, it'll make a good shot."

"OK!"

She walked slowly across the bridge, talking into the camera about the stormy history of the town. And, when she reached the other side she sauntered even more slowly along the flower-bedecked bank.

"Pick some of the flowers, Julie," Ben suggested, manoeuvring the mike to make sure he'd pick up the tone of her voice. "Describe them — take a sniff of them. Let's get a 'back to your ancestors soil' feel about it, OK?"

"And keep more to your left," Jack's instruction came. "It gives me a better angle on the castle."

With a smile, Julie did as the two men asked and stooped low to gather some of the pretty purple flowers at her feet. But then, as she straightened up, something caught her eye — a gleam of gold glistened dully in the sunlight and, inquisitively, she bent down again to take a closer look.

It was a gold locket and she picked it up to examine it more closely. But then, as she did so, she frowned, and her blue eyes darkened. She'd seen this locket somewhere before! There was something oddly familiar about it, and the single initial engraved inside the heart was familiar, too! Helga wore a locket like this, and the initial was the same. Julie shook her head dismissively. How could it be Helga's when she wasn't even in Uj? When she was far away at the convent, nursing a high temperature!

Still in her crouched position, Julie stared hard at the locket and her frown deepened. She rubbed a hand across the back of her neck where her hair had started to prickle and, still gazing down at the locket, a strange feeling of foreboding had suddenly crept around her.

"What's the matter?" Jan's voice called out to her from the other side of the bridge.

Julie straightened up and squinted

across at him, her expression wary. "I don't know," she called back, "but I think you'd better come and have a look at this!"

Jan covered the ground in seconds and, as he reached her side, Julie held out the palm of her hand and exposed the locket. "Do you recognise it, Jan?"

When he didn't answer she asked slowly, "It couldn't possibly be Helga's, could it?"

Jan looked down at the fine, gold chain, his gut contracting and his dark eyes turning suddenly to stone.

"It certainly looks like Helga's — "

"Yes, it does," Julie concurred quietly. "She wears it all the time! I've never known her to take it off." She glanced anxiously up at him, adding, "Do you think she may have followed us here after all?"

His eyes flickered back to the chain, fearing the worst and he hesitated — just fractionally — before he muttered, "She was here — last night — she wanted to see me about something. I met her not far from here, near the castle."

"Last night? But what did she want to see you about? And why didn't she let anyone know she was coming?"

"Because she didn't want anyone else to know about it."

"Not even Dieter?"

"Especially not Dieter."

Julie shook her head, bewildered. "Well, in that case, it's perhaps as well it was us that found the locket — even though it was a million to one chance."

Jan nodded slowly, turning abruptly to signal to the other two to come over and join them. Then he bent down to examine the ground, kicking some of it over with his foot.

His mind raced. Abruptly, he turned his narrowed eyes back to Julie. Murmuring, his voice flat and colourless, and even the half-smile seeming an effort. "So it begins."

Julie glanced quickly up at him.

"What begins? What do you mean?"

He looked at her for a long time, a strange expression on his face, then he said quietly, "We must watch every step we take from now on."

Julie was suddenly scared. "Why, what's happened? And what did you and Helga talk about last night?"

"I haven't time to tell you now."

"But I want to know." Julie insisted. "If I have to watch my step I'll need to know why — and from what."

"I'll explain later. Come on, let's get back to the inn." With his hand on her arm Jan started to lead her towards the bridge.

"Do you think Dieter may have found out that Helga was here?" she asked as they hurried over it and made their way back to the inn.

He shrugged. "I don't know for sure, but I wouldn't be surprised. All I am sure about is the fact that I have to try to find her — and I hope it's not too late."

They reached the inn and, up in

her room, he bent to kiss her lightly on the cheek. "Keep the door locked tight and, while we're gone, pack up your things and be ready to leave in a hurry, OK?"

Julie gave a brief, perplexed nod and Jan threw her a comforting smile.

"Don't worry," he went on softly, "I know what I'm doing. We'll be back before you know it." He pecked her cheek again, adding, "I'll see you later."

Jan beckoned with his head for Jack and Ben to follow him and, as soon as they were back downstairs, he explained the situation to them. Then, checking with the man at the desk, but not able to discover the whereabouts of either Dieter or any of Jantner's men, they went outside into the street.

Jan was sure that the girl was in deep trouble. He could only think that someone must have overheard their conversation last night when they met up by the castle but, who that someone could be, was beyond Jan. He knew it couldn't have been Dieter himself, because he'd made sure he was safely in his room before he'd set out to meet Helga at the castle.

Jan felt the tension growing in him as he checked his handgun. He knew Jantner's small army of rebels were well-armed, but he knew also that they were amateurs — more accustomed to a rifle than an automatic weapon. And, like most professionals, he was nervous of amateurs.

He looked over to the two men. "Ready?"

They nodded. "Ready."

Jan stuffed some spare ammunition into his pocket and the three men headed southwards towards the river.

★ ★ ★

From his window at the inn, Dieter nodded in satisfaction as he heard Jantner's quiet murmur, "They're heading downstream."

"So I see."

145

Jantner smiled, his tall, thin frame turning to face Dieter. "My men are everywhere. They will obey me. The Pole will not see another day — and my son is eager for my forgiveness."

Dieter nodded again, a sullen, brooding anger burning within him. When Jantner had arrived in Uj in the small hours of this morning and told Dieter of his son's and Helga's treachery, he had done well to make up for lost time. Now she was silenced, and Sometski must be silenced, too. He was the only one left who knew of his secret.

He knew Sometski had closed his eyes to a lot of his business, but that was only because he'd had no proof. Now it looked as if he had that proof! She must have given him the papers — they hadn't found them on her body, nor in her room at Jantner's brother's house.

Dieter Bermann's eyes narrowed. Had she wanted the Pole so much that she would risk everything? If that was so, then it was too bad for the both of them. Her desire for Sometski had signed his death warrant. Poor Helga — she had also become greedy, but she had underestimated Dieter Bermann.

He glanced at the Rumanian by his side. "Your men were foolish to be so careless, they could have got rid of her somewhere else."

Jantner remained unmoved. "They thought it best — the river is fast-flowing."

"I know that, you fool, but there are many shallows. Why do you think he is following it?"

Jantner remained unimpressed. "What difference does it make if he does find her? He will be dead soon."

"Your men were reckless to take such a chance so close to the town, they may have been seen. And suppose she has had time to tell the English girl, too? One of your men told me he had seen Helga coming out of the inn before she went back to your brother's place."

"Then we can take care of the

English girl, too."

Dieter glared at the tall, impassive Rumanian. "That might be unwise just yet," he said coldly. "If anything should happen to her, that could be the end for us. Her father has influence, he would expose us on every TV channel there is! All our hard work would be ruined."

"You worry too much."

Bermann eyed the man narrowly. "That may be so, but you had better make sure of Sometski — he has grown very fond of the Stiller girl." Dieter Bermann paused, carefully lighting a cheroot before continuing sourly, "Anyway, you must control your people a little more, they must not be so careless in future."

They fell silent and Dieter considered the situation uneasily. He knew that Jantner had not succeeded in winning over all the groups of rebels that were around. Many did not trust him. Many were already too suspicious of his ambitions.

Dieter frowned somberly. If Jantner wasn't careful, his people could make trouble for him.

The German pursed his lips. The Rumanian was beginning to be a nuisance. He would have to find some way of dispensing with him. And now there was also the English girl to reckon with. Then he smiled to himself. The English girl could be seen to later.

"Remember, nothing must happen to the girl — yet."

Jantner smiled, looking beyond the river to a point in the distance. "I understand."

Dieter thought of Jan Sometski. There was no doubt he would soon work out their little game — he was far too clever to miss a trick. Then he smiled again, thinking silently to himself. "Well, Jan, my brave and foolish friend, at least you will have one thing to thank old Dieter for, you will soon be reunited with your beautiful Anna!"

Jan and the other two men followed the river's course for almost two miles. Would they find Helga somewhere along these banks? And, if they did, would she still be alive? He frowned knowing in his heart that that was already becoming a very faint hope.

Suddenly, Jack stopped, turning back to Jan and pointing to the undergrowth. "That doesn't look so good, Jan," he whispered hoarsely. "Look!"

Jan and Ben caught him up, spotting something that had been caught up on an out-jutting rock. They moved nearer. Their faces grim, they recognised the limp, female shape that was lying face-down against it.

As gently as they could, they hauled Helga out of the river and placed her by a tree. And then, when they could do no more for her, they retraced their steps to notify the police.

Jan was sickened. No matter how shallow her life had been, Helga deserved a better end than the callous one she had endured . . .

Alone in her room, Julie Stiller sighed as she threw her belongings into the canvas bag. It hadn't been the sort of day she would have wished for and, as she unlooped her camera from the hook behind the door to pack it in with the rest, she glanced at it in annoyance. The case had been left open and the lens cap was missing. She cursed her carelessness as she hunted for it on the floor and then replaced it.

She glanced at her watch again, wondering anxiously about Jan. It was long past mid-day. Surely, he wouldn't be much longer! With a small frown, she fastened the bag and went downstairs to find something to eat.

"Ah, Miss Stiller," came the man's voice from the bar. "I hope you did not mind my sending up your visitor so early this morning. She seemed so insistent on seeing you."

Julie glanced up in surprise. "My

visitor? I've had no visitor. Did she leave a name?"

The man shook his head. "No, miss. She asked for your room number, that is all."

"Are you sure it was me she asked for?"

"Yes, miss. But perhaps she changed her mind when she found you were still asleep. Perhaps she will call again later today."

He gave a slight bow and went back to his work, leaving Julie wondering who the woman could have been. Helga, perhaps? She doubted it. Helga had never sought her company even at the best of times! Julie shrugged inwardly. It must have been someone else the woman had asked for and the barman had made a mistake.

Dismissing it from her mind, she went into the dining-room and turned her attention to her lunch of fish and rice. Then, when she had eaten, she went back to her room to wait for Jan.

The time seemed to drag and, for something to do she went to look out of the window. The street below was unusually busy this afternoon, with a number of police and military vehicles milling around. She watched them for a while as they went about their duties, her heart sinking as Dieter Bermann spotted her and waved to her from the square. And then, after having a brief word with one of the soldiers, she saw him make his way towards the inn.

Moments later, her heart sank even more as the knock came on her door, knowing, somehow, it was Dieter.

"Julie," his voice came softly from the other side. "May I speak to you, please. I have some rather unfortunate news, I'm afraid."

"What is it? What do you want, Dieter?" she asked quietly, not moving from the window.

"I have news for you about Jan."

"What news? What about Jan?"

"Will you allow me to enter? It is very difficult talking to you like this."

She hesitated, not wanting a repeat of last night's performance. "I want no more trouble from you, Dieter. Jan will be back very soon."

His answer came back very softly. "That is what I have to talk to you about. Please, open the door."

Reluctantly, Julie moved forward and slipped the catch and, when Dieter took a couple of steps inside, he regarded Julie warily. "I see you are suspicious of me."

"Yes I am, Dieter. But Jan will be back any minute so get on with whatever it is you have to say."

The German smiled softly and shook his head. "That is my unfortunate news, I'm afraid. You see, Jan will not be coming back after all."

Julie froze, her eyes wide and staring at the German. "What are you saying, Dieter?"

"A little while ago he went out to look for Helga, didn't he?"

"Has he found her?"

He shook his head slowly. "I do not

know that. Nor do I know why she should come to this place, either." He shrugged, smiling a little, "But we all know what a strange creature Helga is."

"Dieter, please! Get on with what you have to say. What do you mean, Jan will not be coming back? What is your news of him?"

He smiled coldly, taking a step forward but stopping abruptly as her arm came up and barred his way. "I fear it is bad — the worst."

Julie suddenly froze. "How bad?"

"It would appear that the police have found the body of a man resembling Jan Sometski a little while ago, along with his two companions. I have just had it confirmed by one of the patrols."

She stared at the German uncertainly, the fear growing even stronger. "What are you saying?"

"It seems there was some trouble by the river, that is why the military are here in such numbers. It would appear that some of the rebels have come from the mountains to steal what they can from the town, and Jan and the others must have tried — unsuccessfully — to stop them." He paused, his eyes cold and ruthless, continuing softly, "The police are warning all of us. It is very dangerous here for us now, I'm afraid. We must leave soon, and only I can get you home safely."

Stunned and fearful, Julie stared at him as though she was frozen. "It isn't true!" she called to him despairingly. "Jan will be back! I know he will! I don't believe a word of what you say!"

He smiled at her briefly, "It is unimportant whether you believe me or not, little one. I have told you the truth. And now, you must finish your packing. We must all prepare to leave this town by noon tomorrow at the latest. Now lock your door after I leave. I will put a guard outside so that you will sleep in safety tonight."

When he had gone, Julie stood stock still, loneliness and despair overwhelming her, and now fearing everything.

But, if what Dieter said was true, there was nothing she could do except as he asked. And, when sunset tinged the sky and Jan still hadn't returned, Julie's desperation had almost reached fever-pitch. She felt so helpless, able to do nothing. The next couple of hours seemed the longest of her life.

She couldn't sleep, and didn't even try to. Every movement from the street below brought more wakefulness. She was even afraid to look at her watch because, as the time ticked by, she felt even more afraid.

Julie had no idea how long she lay in the muffled silence of her room. But, when she heard the door open softly and the touch of a hand came upon her arm, a scream rose in her throat. The hand came up to her mouth, stifling any sound she tried to make and, as her eyes strained against the darkness, she was suddenly aware of the black shape as it bent over her, forcing her to be still.

His voice came, urgent and whispering,

against her face, "Don't be scared!" Her eyes stared up, wild and afraid. "I'm moving my hand away now, but don't make a sound. Do you hear me?"

Julie nodded stiffly as she recognised Jan's whispered voice, relief that he was safe overwhelming her. And as he took his hand away she gasped for breath. "Jan — Dieter told me — How did you — ?"

"We were ambushed — it's a long story! Anyway, no time to explain now — we haven't much time. But, Julie, you must do as I say!"

Julie nodded again, able now to recognise his handsome features through the blur. "OK," she whispered back, making a move to rise. "The guard. Dieter put a guard on me. How did you — "

Jan put his hands on her shoulders. "I paid for his assistance."

"Are we getting out of here?"

"Yes. But not yet."

"Not yet? When then?"

"We can't leave tonight."

"Why?"

"Trust me and listen carefully. We will get away, I promise you. But first, you must give me some time. They've taken our car so, we'll have to find something else. That's why I need your help."

"What do you want me to do?"

"Tomorrow, when Dieter comes for you, you must act as though you believe I'm dead. Try and act as though you've accepted the situation."

"But — "

"Shh. Don't speak — just listen. I want you to stall for time so that we can get hold of some kind of transport." And when she nodded, he continued again, his whispered voice becoming even more urgent now, "At eleven o'clock, make some excuse and go back towards the river — near to the place where you found the locket, OK?" She nodded again. "The boys and I will be waiting. With any luck we'll have a car and can take the back road out of here and get away over the mountains."

"Jan — " She caught at his arm. "Jan — did you find Helga?"

"I'm afraid we did, but we were too late." He stared down at her, cupping her chin and forcing her to look up. "But it's not going to be too late for us, OK?"

She nodded again, answering in a whisper. "OK."

Grim lines were deepening Jan's mouth. "I'll explain all these things some other time," he said. "What is more important right now is that these next few hours will be dangerous, I don't have to spell it out." He paused for a moment, sighing deeply. "Look, I hate leaving you alone again like this, but I have to. I have no choice if we're to get away safely."

"Can't you try to get a car or something now?"

He shook his head. "No, we've already tried. All the cars are heavily guarded. There are too many men

160

around for us, I'm afraid." His eyes softened a little at her alarmed gaze and he added reassuringly, "Don't worry, we'll make it. It's just that we need more time and, by staying here, you will give it to us. They think I'm dead and I want them to keep on thinking that for the next few hours. If they believed for one minute that one of us was alive they would hunt us down like dogs. Believe me, I know what I'm doing — you must trust me."

"I do." She managed a small smile.

"Good girl!" He smiled briefly, holding her to him for a moment. "Remember, eleven o'clock, at the river!"

"I'll be there."

He kissed her briefly on her lips. "Tomorrow we'll be miles away from here."

Then he was gone as silently as he had come.

★ ★ ★

161

When daylight came next day, Julie got up, washed and dressed, and thankful to find that her door was unguarded, she went down into the dining-room as though all was normal. She glanced at her watch — it was already after eight. Her thoughts drifted to Dieter and of the way he had lied to her yesterday! She despised the man! But Jan was alive and, remembering, she pulled herself quickly together, determined to act out the little game and play her part of the grieving lover. It was vital — their lives depended on it.

Julie smiled at Dieter as he came through the door, hoping she looked suitably subdued — a sentiment she was far from feeling!

"Have you eaten yet?" he asked her.

"No, not yet."

"Have you no appetite this morning?"

She shook her head sadly, looking wide-eyed up at the German. "How can I have now that Jan — ?"

"Come, come, little one. You must

eat. We have a long journey before us and you will need your strength."

"I'm not hungry, Dieter. Perhaps I may have something later."

"Ah, yes, I understand. Grieving takes one's appetite away."

Julie gave a deep sigh, answering calmly, "Yes, it does."

"You look pale, my dear."

Julie nodded, hanging her head. "Yes, I suppose I must. I feel quite sick and ill, Dieter. Perhaps I need a little air." She pressed a hand to her forehead and prayed she looked convincing.

Dieter checked his watch. "Well, we have a little time and I do not want a fainting woman on my hands. Perhaps if you took a walk in the fresh air you would feel a little better."

"I'm — I'm sure I will. It feels so stuffy in here."

Weakly, taking Dieter's arm for assistance, Julie got to her feet and made her way slowly to the door. Opening it, she threw a frail, little smile back to him and went outside, walking slowly towards the square. She must keep a level-head and she measured her stride, quelling the urge to run and knowing that Dieter's eyes were following her as she pretended to wipe away a tear.

Another surreptitious glance at her watch told her it was now ten-thirty! Half an hour to go!

She looked over to the row of trucks and cars. Less than fifty yards away from her, Dieter and a couple of Jantner's men were already preparing to leave. She watched as they piled bags and cases into the boots and Julie shivered suddenly, her eyes like ice. He must have ordered Helga killed last night — and perhaps, Jan and Jack and Ben, too! How many more would have to die before they were safely out of here?

Slowly and deliberately, she headed towards the river, glancing back at Dieter. The muscles of her stomach were already tight, and the adrenalin flowed. She felt a little like a condemned prisoner making a bid at escape — which, of course, she was!

Dieter glanced across expressionlessly and she smiled at him. Thankfully, he seemed not to notice her direction and, with an air of feigned indifference, Julie strolled on. It was the longest distance she had ever walked.

At the river's edge Julie looked back once more at Dieter, but he was now intent on the overseeing of the vehicles. She smiled a little, her hopes lifting as she increased her pace and made her way more quickly along the river's bank. Then, when she had reached the spot where she found Helga's locket, she looked desperately one way and then the other for a glimpse of Jan.

"This way, Julie!"

"Jan! Where are you?"

"Here! This way!"

She turned quickly in the direction of the voice. Some feet away, the dark nose of a jeep was just discernible through a tangle of trees. As she made her way towards it, she recognised the blurred faces of Jack and Ben in the back.

Reaching it, she jumped into the passenger seat, feeling Jan's arm reach out to steady her and haul her inside. And then they were off — Jan engaging the gears and heading the jeep along the path.

Within minutes, they were away from the river bank and driving swiftly away from Dieter and the others — out towards the mountains.

At first the drive was quiet, passing no one on their way, but then Ben held up his hand. "Jan — behind us!"

Jan glanced in the mirror. Behind them like specks of dust, three cars were already in pursuit.

"It didn't take them long!" Jan muttered. "How many do you reckon?"

"Three cars — four men in each at a guess."

"Shall we turn off?" Ben asked. "Make for the main highway?"

"No. We'll keep going this way! I

know these mountains like the back of my hand — we'll lose them sooner or later." Jan glanced at Julie, ordering, "Keep your head low if they come any nearer — it could get rough."

It did get rough. Twelve against four made unreasonable odds. There was the crack of gun fire and, instinctively, they crouched low and soon, the air around them was echoing to the sound of bullets and Julie ducked even lower as one whistled past her ear, splintering the mirror on the wing.

Keeping their heads down, Jan somehow managed to maintain a fair distance between themselves and the hostile cars behind. By now, Julie had lost track of time. The only thing she knew for certain was that the bullets were far too close for any peace of mind.

But then, suddenly, all was quiet and, raising her head warily Julie looked up. "What's happened?"

Jan grinned slightly. "I think we're losing them!"

True enough, when Julie looked behind again she could see that the pursuing cars were definitely dropping back, and not seeming to make any further effort to catch them up.

Straightening up in the seat, Julie breathed a sigh of relief. "But why are they giving up so soon?"

"Who knows? They probably haven't enough fuel for the mountains and daren't risk it." He looked back again and smiled grimly. "Anyway, who cares? We're losing them right enough — we're OK now."

Julie looked behind her again. There were only two cars in sight now, and they were dropping farther and farther away as the gradient increased between them. She turned to Jan, smiling faintly in her relief.

"Well, I can't say I'm sorry that's over," she said. "But now what happens?"

Jan relaxed a little, leaning back against the seat and turning his head so that he could look at her straight.

"We'll get these mountains behind us as quickly as we can. Then we'll make for the base at Tulcea before Dieter has time to refuel."

They drove on in silence. There was no sign of Dieter or Jantner's men now, and Julie was glad of it. Around her, as though there was nothing else in the world, the silent infinity of mountain and forest wrapped around them with not a sign of a human soul, just endless shapes of white and brown, green and grey, rolling endlessly and timelessly before them.

Three hours of hard, fast driving was beginning to take its toll on Jan. The dark circles around his eyes were relieved only by the redness of his blood-shot eyes and Julie began to worry. He couldn't possibly keep up this pace without relief, but when any of them offered to take his place, he adamantly refused.

Soon, the mountain roads were giving way to scrubby fields and Julie knew they were coming to their journey's end. In the distance, she saw a low, single-storied building with a wind sock flapping in the breeze and, realising it was the base, her heart lifted. As they pulled up outside a door and the American came out to greet them, she felt that she had never been so glad to see anybody in all her life.

8

JAN SOMETSKI stretched his long legs before the glowing fire in the O'Reilly's living-room and sighed contentedly.

Lilly had done them proud, cooking the four of them the best meal they'd had for over a week. He thought of Julie, and wondered what she was making of all the things that had happened. She hadn't complained — not a word. But how different she must feel now from the fresh, smiling girl he'd first seen step off the plane at Budapest airport. He wondered morosely whether she regretted her trip and whether she still trusted his judgement after what had happened to Helga.

He heard the door open behind him and looked round, half-expecting it to be Mac, but it seemed he was still chatting to Jack and Ben in the kitchen and it was Julie who came in, bringing him a mug of coffee.

He smiled a little as she handed it to him. "Your trip hasn't turned out exactly how you imagined, has it?"

Julie shrugged slightly. "I'm not complaining."

"Look, I'm sorry I've got you into this mess," he murmured apologetically. "It wasn't intended."

"I know that. Forget it."

"You can't say it's been a success."

"Oh, I don't know. I've learned a lot and I've certainly seen more than I bargained for — like almost being shot out of the mountains. What more could a girl ask for? And, on top of all that, I've managed to get some filming done — if we ever manage to get back home to have it processed, that is. I think I can safely say that it's been quite an experience."

Jan nodded his head. "I suppose you could say that."

When she went back to the others

in the kitchen, he lay his head hack against the sofa, bone-weary tired. He sighed again, rubbing a hand across his eyes. He knew it wasn't over yet! Dieter Bermann was not going to give up on him so easily — he knew too much now! Jan was also remembering something else. Something Helga had said that night at the castle. She had told him that the money would be arriving on the only plane due into the base tonight — the plane he had intended to use to get Julie back to home and safety. If only he could get his hands on those blasted papers!

He got up briskly and strode into Mac's office and radio-room, pulling up a cane chair and talking into a radio for several minutes. When he'd finished, he turned to see Julie standing just a couple of feet behind him.

"I feel partly to blame for all this trouble, you know," she murmured.

He glanced at her, surprised. "Why? What have you to blame yourself for?"

She shook her head doubtfully.

"If I hadn't decided to come on this trip, Dieter would probably still be in Hamburg or wherever, and Helga would still be alive."

She held his gaze, seeing the look of compassion come into his eyes. He smiled bleakly, saying quietly, "That's a crazy thing to say. None of this is any of your fault. It would have happened sooner or later. I would have come back on another trip with Dieter anyway, and I would have had to face the day of reckoning with him before much longer." He turned away from her for a moment but not before Julie had seen the unmistakable glimmer of pain in his eyes. "And as for Helga." He sighed deeply. "She knew she was cutting a fine line."

"Yes."

"Anyway — " He stood up briskly, swinging his legs from around the chair. "Let's join the — "

But Jan got no further. Suddenly, the door burst open and Mac's head appeared round it, "Jan! We've got company! Looks like Bermann!"

Jan swung round, giving a sort of grunting expellation of his breath. Then he moved, very fast, and the next thing Julie knew she was following him out of the room and to the windows at the front of the house. Her heart sank like a stone when she saw the two trucks, coming at speed and less than a mile away. It sank even more as she recognised the car, knowing it was likely to be Dieter at the wheel, with Jantner sitting beside him in the passenger seat.

Their stunned silence was suddenly broken by the crackle of the base's radio, "Redbird to Base! Request permission to land! Over!"

Mac glanced uncertainly at Jan, "They're coming in. And I told them to carry on to Bucharest. They must be mad! What do we do now?"

Jan said nothing for a moment, staring impassively at the sky. Then he said grimly, "Better bring them in."

"You realise what you're saying?"

"Can't be helped, we'll just have to risk it — they could be short of fuel by now."

"Right! Pity both the chopper's are still at Galati though. We could have got you out of here in time."

Mac sat at the radio and flicked some switches, speaking into the mouthpiece with an aggressive urgency.

"Base to Redbird! Make landing from South! Repeat! Make landing from South! Over!"

"Redbird to Base! Approaching from South! Three passengers! E.T.A. fifteen minutes. Redbird Out!"

Mac put down the mouthpiece and glanced at a list of names on his desk before looking back at Jan.

"Three passengers," he confirmed. "They'll be Stiller and two Dutch businessmen."

Jan felt Julie's hand catch his sleeve as she looked quickly at Mac. "Did you say Stiller? My father? Is my father coming here today?"

Mac nodded. "That's right. And two other guys."

Jan smiled grimly. "Sounds like it may turn out to be quite a party."

Lilly O'Reilly came into the office with more coffee. "I've a feeling we're all going to need this before this night is through," she commented drily.

Jan took a mug and went over to look out of the window and, when the two women had left the room, Mac went over to join him. They looked out at the far side of the runway where the car and the truck had pulled in, and Jan estimated roughly how many men were in each vehicle.

Mac lit a cigar. "Are you going to tell me what's going on?" he asked. "What's Bermann up to, sitting out there like a sphinx?"

"He's making sure we don't board the plane when it arrives."

"Why? What's his game?"

Jan gave an expressive shrug. "Dieter needs that plane more than we do. I doubt he'll make his move before it

177

lands, then, if my guesses are right, he'll meet his contacts because, without them his whole deal goes down the tube. Besides, he'll be saving us for extra insurance. He thinks I have Helga's papers."

"What papers?"

Jan told Mac about Dieter's activities and Helga's written proof of them. Of how he'd seen for himself the two incriminating documents that gave the signatures of Dieter, Jantner, and the arms and drugs dealers. When he had finished, Mac whistled through his teeth.

"If that's all true, then he's in pretty deep. But why have it down in black and white? I would have thought Bermann would have had more sense than that!"

"That's probably Jantner's idea. There's no trust between either of them and it's probably his life insurance."

"And Bermann knows that you know all that?"

"Yes." Jan took a sip of his coffee

and then his gaze went back to the waiting car. It stood eerily still, clear of the runway, its headlights glinting dully in the evening light. Then, suddenly, his face stilled, his breath exhaling sharply between his teeth.

Jan stared out at the car. "Mac," he ordered urgently, "Get Jack and Ben — and anyone else you can find! Bermann's gone! He's not in the car!"

In the kitchen, Julie rinsed the coffee mugs, praying silently that the plane carrying her father would land safely, and that the expected trouble from Dieter Bermann would turn out to be nothing but a figment of Jan's imagination.

It was too much to hope, of course. Within minutes she could hear the plane's engines as it circled the base. She pulled the blind to one side and looked up at the sky and then, moments later, she saw the small, silver plane touch down and taxi along the runway.

She glanced out again, a small

cry escaping as Jantner's small army of rebels came into focus. Within minutes, they were everywhere and, as the plane's door opened, the first face she saw was that of her father's.

She raced towards the door with Lilly following behind. But, as she pulled it open she stopped in her tracks as her way was blocked by the broad bulk of Dieter Bermann. His arm barred her flight, and his eyes fixed coldly on her as ten seconds of tense, fearful silence fell between them like a shroud.

"What's all the hurry, little one." Bermann's tone was menacing.

He pushed her back inside the room, twisting her arm around her back. He beckoned to one of Jantner's men who was waiting outside, and who, to Julie's horror, forced both herself and Lilly back into the room. Dieter held her fast while the man tied Lilly to a chair. Then, when he felt she was secure, he reached inside his jacket for a length of rope, grabbing hold of Julie and forcing her hands behind her back. Then with painful proficiency, he tied them up behind her.

"Now, you can do something for me, my pretty one," Dieter said, satisfied she could not move and pushing the door open with his foot before forcing her outside.

Keeping his head down, Jan skirted around the back of the building until he was out of sight of Jantner's men. He pressed himself against a wall as Dieter came out with Julie, reining his impulse to lunge when he saw the gun at Julie's back. He swore silently, cursing himself for giving the German even a hair's breadth of chance.

He half-turned his head towards the plane. Jantner and some of his men had encircled it, holding Julie's father at gun point while the pilot was forced to refuel. Further on, he could see Jantner in deep conversation with the other two men. Then he moved cautiously, ducking the wire strands that separated the building from the runway, making for the luggage truck that stood just a few yards from the plane.

For a few tense moments all was quiet as Jan planned his action. Briefly, he caught a glimpse of Mac at the window with Ben and Jack, and wondered how they'd managed to escape Jantner's men. He also saw the glint of their guns as they levelled them towards the runway. With his stomach churning, Jan moved silently round the back of the plane and towards Dieter, stooping low under its belly and using it for cover.

"Let her go!" he heard Stiller call out.

And Dieter's quiet answer came, "She's coming with me. Your daughter in exchange for two little pieces of paper. A fair bargain, ja?"

"Let my daughter go first, Bermann—"

Then Colin Stiller's protests were stilled suddenly as a fist came out and sent him to the ground.

"Dad!" Julie yelled, trying to pull away from Dieter.

But the German held her fast, "Not

so fast, English girl. Be patient." Then laughing and sounding very confident, he called out now in German to the Dutchmen, "Did you bring the money?"

"Of course!" one of them replied. "Would we come this far without it?"

"Give it to Jantner, he knows what to do."

"Not until we see the merchandise."

"The men will load it on to the plane."

"We'll keep the money until they do. Until we're all safely back on the plane."

"It is not in the deal that I go back with you. The exchange is to be completed here. My arrangements to leave have already been made."

"The deal has changed. You must come with us."

"Very well. It makes no difference to me." He addressed the pilot. "Have you almost finished?"

Jan knew now that there was very little time. He bent down, lowering his gun and moving forward. His eyes never left the German as he crawled beneath the plane, edging cautiously towards him.

Then, summoning all his energy, he sprang, lunging blindly forward and sending Dieter's gun hand into the air as he brought the butt of his revolver down against his head.

All hell broke loose then. Mac and the other two opened fire from the house, and Jan kicked Dieter's gun away with his foot before trying to pull Julie out of harm's way.

But, Julie, realising she was free from Dieter's hold, had already twisted away. With her eyes dilated and fear for her father uppermost in her thoughts, she started to run towards him. Slowly, instinctively, the German, winded and white faced, rolled over and snatched up the gun again, pointing it directly at her fleeing form.

Jan, anticipating the action, flung himself forward and kicked out at the German, hearing the sharp snap of Bermann's wrist as his boot made contact. Dieter let out a scream, but still held on to the gun and, turning back to Jan, he raised the barrel to his face.

Without stopping to think, Jan fired. Then, suddenly, the German fell into a crumpled mass on the ground.

Jan looked up, glancing towards the plane. He saw Julie with her father and heard her calling his name. Then everything seemed still. He could hear no more. He was aware of nothing now except the dull thud of the bullet that had hit him, spinning him backwards for at least three feet.

He heard voices all around him and he tried to answer, but no words came. Then there was the sound of helicopter's rotors hovering above his head. But perhaps it was a dream, because it was all so dark. He was conscious of nothing now as a great wall of oblivion closed in around him.

9

COLIN STILLER looked across at his daughter as her shaking fingers struggled to spoon a speck of dust from the whirling, creamy swirls in the coffee-cup. She certainly hadn't been kidding when she had told him how much she cared for Jan Sometski. Sitting there, in the waiting-room of Bucharest's main hospital, Stiller knew that he had finally lost her. But, from what he had learned of the man, he would have no need to worry.

He patted her hand. "Try not to worry so much. We know he's already out of danger now. Just a couple of more days and then we can fly him home."

She put the spoon down, her movements brusque with nervousness. "But, Dad, he almost died! Jan almost died saving my life!"

There was a short pause before Stiller said quietly, "I know. And he saved all our lives by radioing Bucharest when he did."

Julie shuddered violently as she got to her feet to move restlessly across to the window. She stood silently for a moment looking out. She'd had three weeks of hell! Three weeks of not being able to sleep, eat, or think coherently while she'd waited for Jan to recover his strength. They had told her more than once he was improving, but she'd been too afraid to believe it! It was foolish to be so neurotic she told herself. Foolish and silly. She wasn't helping anyone acting this way — especially Jan!

But how could she help it when she remembered the violent events of three weeks ago? When she had sat with him in the helicopter to Bucharest, being told by the doctor that he had been very lucky indeed — and that the bullet from Jantner's gun had missed his heart by a mere fraction of an inch?

Standing here in the waiting-room, the silence seemed to be closing in on her and she walked around, her hand gripping even more tightly around the leather bag that was slung across her shoulder.

Her mind drifted again to the man who had been lying so desperately ill in his hospital bed. Three weeks ago, the shooting at the air base had hit the world's headlines. The whole rotten story of Dieter Bermann and the Rumanian, Franz Jantner, had broken out in a roar of public outrage.

As Jan had lain on the red earth of the base, the place had been suddenly surrounded. It had been difficult for the rebels to escape. They had tried to flee, scattering back into the mountains like fleas on a dog, but armed militia had flushed them out and their panic-stricken attempts to break loose had inevitably been cut off.

Jantner was finished — the Dutchmen, too! They hadn't stood a chance of getting away.

It had taken less than an hour for the police to round them up. They had been disarmed and bundled into the helicopters to be despatched to Bucharest, and now the Rumanian was awaiting trial for the attempted murder of Jan Sometski.

Julie bit her lip, remembering. She would never forget seeing Jantner's gun aimed at Jan. She had tried to warn him, but he hadn't heard her. And by the time she had reached him he was already on the ground.

Her hand tightened again around her bag. "Oh, Jan," she uttered silently. "Please — please — don't leave me now! Please! Please! Come back to me!"

★ ★ ★

Jan's eyes flickered open. He looked around the room, taking in the whitewashed walls, the vase of flowers on the locker at his side and the small figure in white that was seated by the

189

window. He tried to move again but still found it difficult. "Julie?"

The nurse got up from her chair, moving to his side and her kindly, intelligent brown eyes flickering to the dials that had been monitoring his vital functions. "Welcome back, Mr Sometski. I'll tell Julie you're awake. She's been waiting so long to see you."

When the nurse showed her in, Julie's eyes looked across the room to where Jan lay, then softly, she moved to stand by his bed. She looked down at Jan's sleeping face. His breathing was even and regular and a wide strip of bandage was wound across his shoulder where the bullet had been removed. Beneath the bandage, and around the edges, Julie could see the deep bluish marks of bruising and, as she glanced at his face, his hair seemed darker than ever against the white of the pillow.

Her hand reached out, as though of its own accord, and touched his brow. "Jan," she whispered, "Jan, are you awake?"

He stirred, turning his head and, his dark eyelashes flickering momentarily, he opened his eyes. "Julie?"

"How are you feeling?"

He turned on his back. "A bit groggy, but I'm told I'll live."

"You've had me worried sick."

"Have I?" He reached for her hand. "Sorry, love, I didn't mean to."

She smiled. "Don't be silly. I'm just grateful to see you looking so much better again."

He gave a little laugh. "Thanks."

He moved his mending body into a more comfortable position and looked at Julie, acknowledging silently what she must have been through the last couple of weeks. The knowledge brought anger to him and, for a moment, he looked away, soured by the memory of Dieter Bermann and seeing the German again in his mind's eye — at his feet.

Then he turned back, waiting a moment before asking more seriously.

"What happened back there? It's a bit blurry to me yet. They tell me they got Jantner."

"Yes, they did. And the Dutchmen. It's all over, Jan."

"Is your Dad OK?"

"He's fine. He's outside now and would like to see you. He wants to thank you for saving my life — as I do."

Jan grinned. "Any time." Then his grin faded a little. "Has he told you why he came out here? Didn't he think you were safe with me?"

Julie smiled. "It wasn't that," she answered quietly. "It seems that Dieter Bermann's game was already up according to some information that was leaked to Dad's office. And then, by coincidence, when my letter happened to reach him on the very day that Helga was murdered . . . Well, he made arrangements to fly out and take me home. He knew Dieter had to be the one behind Helga's murder, and of the hatred he always felt for you. He was afraid you would be next, and that I would be left alone. Anyway, that's all over with now." She smiled briefly, gathering up her bag and opening it to bring out two pieces of paper. "Look, I have a present for you."

"What is it?"

"Can't you guess?"

Jan stared at the papers, reaching out to take them and opening them up. His eyes scanned the contents then he turned, unbelieving, back to Julie. "Where did you find them?"

"You'll never believe it!"

"Try me!" Jan put his hand over hers and squeezed it. "You should know by now that I'll believe anything you tell me." It was an instant bond. With mock severity he asked again, "Now, are you going to tell me or do I have to wait until we're on our honeymoon and worm it out of you? Where did you find these papers?"

Julie looked down at his hand and felt his warmth. She loved him, and he loved her. No matter what happened from now on, nothing would ever be the same again for either of them.

She gave a little shrug. "They were in my camera case."

He stared at her incredulous. "In your camera case?"

"Yes." She swallowed, glancing at his darkened face before she went on. "When I went to our hotel after we left you here, the police had left all my things with my father." She swallowed again. "They told me later that, while we were on the plane, they cleared up the mess at the base. They stripped the car and the trucks. Naturally, they found our stuff, including my camera, and sent it on. And, when I opened my camera case, there they were . . . " She hesitated, remembering the German girl again. "Helga must have put them there on the night she died . . . She must have come into my room while I was asleep and hidden them in my camera case."

They fell silent for a moment, sitting quietly holding hands and Jan letting

Julie's words sink in. He smiled a little sadly. Helga had been clever. Who would have thought of looking in Julie's camera case? Certainly, Dieter hadn't! Nor Jantner!

"Poor Helga," he murmured at last while reaching for Julie's hand.

"Yes, poor Helga."

"Well, at least we've got the proof to put Jantner away for a long time. The others, too."

"Yes. These papers are only copies, of course. The police have the originals. They're too damning to risk another loss. But, I — I wanted you to see them."

"I'm glad I have."

A soft tap came on the door and they both looked up. Jan grinned a little ruefully. "More visitors by the sound of it."

"It's probably Dad. Shall I tell him to go away?"

"No, of course not. I'd like to see him."

"And it could be the doctor coming

to drive me away from you."

"Wild horses couldn't do that. Better see who it is."

The door opened and Colin Stiller came into the room, walking over to Jan and shaking his hand warmly.

"I owe you a great deal, Sometski," he said quietly. "Words will never be enough."

Jan gave a small grin. "It was a pleasure, sir."

They shook hands again and then Colin winked at Julie and went back to the door, opening it a little wider.

"There's someone else waiting patiently to thank you." He grinned. And, as he gestured, little Karol entered, wearing the broadest grin Jan had ever seen.

The boy hobbled farther into the room. His leg was bound and splintered, and the crutches under his arms were far too tall for him but, when he reached their side, he held out his hand proudly for Julie to take.

"I much better," he said, shyly.

He beamed at Julie. He was used to

seeing her. She had called in to see him on her daily visits to Jan. And she knew all about the skin grafts to his leg — and that, before too long, he would be as right as rain.

"Well, I'm glad, Karol," Jan was saying, grinning as he gingerly took the boy's hand. "Have you got many stitches?"

"Many stitch, yes? You have many, too?"

Jan laughed. "I don't know how many I have. We'll have to take a look sometime."

★ ★ ★

Four weeks later, sitting at a table in one of York's more intimate restaurants, Julie twirled the stem of her wine glass looking across at Jan. He was thinking how beautiful she looked tonight, with her shining hair catching the light like a halo and her blue eyes sparkling. She was more important to him now than anything else.

He took hold of her hand, squeezing it for a moment before taking a sip of his wine, then looking across as his eyes searched her face. "Darling, have you thought any more of what I asked you yesterday?"

Julie smiled. "Of course, I have. And I've decided that I would rather like to be the wife of a Scottish laird."

"Well, hardly that. And it's miles away from anywhere, you know. Do you think you would miss having people around?"

"No, I don't think so — I've been thinking mainly about how many children we would have, and what a marvellous amount of space there would be for them to grow up in." She smiled softly at him. "No, Jan, I can't think of anywhere else I'd rather be."

"Not even Uj-Moldova?"

She shook her head. "No, not even there. It's a pretty place and I'm glad I've seen it, but it's no longer a part of me — or my family. This is our home now." Julie smiled and squeezed his hand, "Now, my love, finish your drink and let's go back to your flat and take Oonie over to my father's house. After all, she's the one who will be washing his socks from now on. Besides — " she said as she gave his hand another squeeze, "It's been a few hours since you last kissed me."

Jan Sometski felt at peace then — real peace. It was the same peace he had felt the very first time he had gone into the mountains. He took her hand and brought it gently to his lips. Tomorrow they would be married, and he and Julie would be going home.

THE END